Playing With Fire

THE FIRST FREAK HOUSE TRILOGY
#2

C.J. ARCHER

Other books by C.J. Archer:

The Wrong Girl (The 1st Freak House Trilogy #1)

The Medium (Emily Chambers Spirit Medium #1)

Possession (Emily Chambers Spirit Medium #2)

Evermore (Emily Chambers Spirit Medium #3)

Her Secret Desire (Lord Hawkesbury's Players #1)

Scandal's Mistress (Lord Hawkesbury's Players #2)

To Tempt The Devil (Lord Hawkesbury's Players #3)

Honor Bound (The Witchblade Chronicles #1)

Kiss Of Ash (The Witchblade Chronicles #2)

The Charmer (Assassins Guild #1)

Courting His Countess

Redemption

Surrender

The Mercenary's Price

CHAPTER 1

Frakingham House, Hertfordshire, December 1888

"There are simply too many men," Sylvia announced. "We need another woman. A single one, preferably of middle age for Uncle's sake." She sighed and scanned the piece of paper in her hand for the third time since joining Jack, Samuel and me on the front lawn of Frakingham House. Her sigh said it all. It would seem she couldn't conjure a spare unattached female from her list of invitees.

"I'm not sure your uncle would care one way or another," I said, dipping my paintbrush into the blob of indigo on my palette. "Is he looking for a wife?"

"I'm not trying to marry him off, Hannah. I want a perfect dinner party, and you can't have the perfect dinner party with an unbalanced number of ladies and gentlemen."

"Are even numbers an absolute must for the perfect dinner party?" Jack asked, twirling a dueling pistol around his finger. It wasn't loaded, nor was Samuel's, but Sylvia did not take her gaze off it.

I'd made the two men hold them and stand a little apart, their backs to one another. My painting was going to be titled *Pistols at Dawn* and have a dramatic, swirling sky, but I

5

wasn't a very good artist. It was particularly difficult to render the house in the background since it was still covered in scaffolding.

"Honestly, Jack," Sylvia said with a shake of her head that made her blonde curls bounce, "I can't believe you have to ask me that." She pulled the fur collar of her coat up to her ears and huddled into it. "On second thought, perhaps I can believe it, all things considered."

Jack caught the pistol's handle, halting the twirling. His mouth flattened and his gaze flashed in Samuel's direction. Fortunately the meaning behind her words appeared to be lost on our resident hypnotist. Either that or he was too polite to ask for an explanation. He simply remained standing side-on to me, his pistol at his chest in the pose I'd asked him to assume for my painting. I knew that Sylvia was referring to Jack's past as an orphan living on the London streets. Dinner party etiquette was not something he was overly familiar with. Nor was I. As the orphan daughter of servants and living most of my eighteen years in Lord Wade's attic, I was lucky that I had received food at all. Parties had occurred downstairs, out of my hearing and sight, and very much out of my world.

"Tell them, Samuel," Sylvia said, sniffing. Her nose had gone red from the cold, and I was surprised she was still with us. She hated being outdoors now that autumn had slipped into a freezing winter.

I, on the other hand, loved the cool air whispering across my warm skin, and I couldn't abide wearing gloves. Jack too. As fire starters, we didn't feel the cold like normal people.

"Samuel?" Sylvia prompted when he didn't answer. "Do not tell me that dinner parties are foreign to you too. How can that be? *You're* a gentleman."

The implication being that Jack was not. Samuel made no indication that he understood the slight, which indeed confirmed that he was a gentleman in every sense. Not that it mattered. Jack wasn't listening. He cocked his head to the side and frowned, intent on something in the distance. I looked about, but all seemed as it should be. The foreman stood at the base of the scaffolding in discussion with one of his workers, and two other men tapped away at the newly rebuilt turret. They'd had to tear down the old one after the fire that ravaged the upper level of the eastern wing had rendered the turret unstable.

The fire that I'd accidentally started.

"I've attended my share of dinner parties," said Samuel, oblivious to Jack's distraction. "Of sorts." Samuel Gladstone had joined us a mere two weeks earlier after leaving the employ of a premier London neurologist as well as his studies at University College. He'd come to the country to conduct hypnosis research, but I'd yet to learn the exact nature of it and why it necessitated him being here, or if it had anything to do with his natural hypnosis ability. He'd been born with a talent for coercing people with little more than his voice and eyes, something which he'd hidden from most people, including his former employer.

"Whatever do you mean?" asked Sylvia.

He rubbed the pistol's ivory handle with his thumb. "Dinner was served, and they were indeed parties."

Sylvia looked to me askance, and I shrugged. I hadn't any idea what he was saying either. "What was your mother's opinion on the matter of equal numbers of gentlemen and ladies?" she asked.

He looked up sharply. "My mother?"

"Was it not your mother who hosted the dinners?"

He gave us a lopsided grin, turning his angelic face into something more like that of a naughty boy. He was terribly handsome with his fair hair and blue eyes. Not at all like Jack whose darkly brooding good looks and stormy green eyes were more devilish. I hoped to catch that contrast on canvas.

"My mother had nothing to do with the dinner parties I attended," Samuel said. "I was away at school and university while she was being hostess to her friends. I endured one or two while on holidays, but mostly I avoided them. Mother's parties were a little more...formal than what I was used to."

"Oh? In what way were your parties informal?"

Samuel had an amiable face, and he smiled often, but it didn't always reach his eyes where shadows lurked at the edges. This was one of those times. "Never mind, Sylvia. I don't want to shock you."

She bristled. "I'm not easily shocked."

"There are some things a lady shouldn't hear."

"Then why bring it up at all?"

He flinched then bowed. "I apologize."

She made a sound through her nose and turned away from him, cutting him in the rudest manner. It was rather unfair since *she'd* been the one to bring up the subject of party etiquette. She may have done it to put Jack in his place, but it had backfired since he wasn't listening, and Samuel had proved to have an elusive past shrouded in mystery too. Sylvia was mostly kind and sweet, but there were times when I wanted to pinch her. Samuel always took her childishness with charm and good grace, which I admired. Where Jack would tease his cousin further, Samuel chose the higher ground.

I didn't know much about him, but I did know that I liked him. I also knew that being born with the ability to hypnotize people had been as much a blessing as a curse for him. He didn't speak often of the past, but I got the distinct feeling he hadn't always used his talent honorably. I was quite sure that he'd changed since then and no longer hypnotized anyone against their wishes.

Jack was not so certain. He'd not *said* he distrusted Samuel, but he tended to avoid him as much as possible. Considering they were of similar age and both had strange natural abilities, I thought it a shame they weren't friends. Perhaps time under the same roof would change that.

"What am I to do?" Sylvia asked, once more checking her list of guests.

"I could bow out," Samuel said. "I have upset the balance in the household, so it's only fair that I be the one to miss out." He glanced at Jack as he said it, but Jack's attention was still drawn to the house.

What was the matter? Everything seemed in order to me. The workmen were busy. The scaffolding looked steady. August Langley was nowhere in sight, presumably in his temporary room working on a new drug. Yet Jack took a step forward, frowned, and seemed to be straining to hear beyond our light chatter.

"Don't be ridiculous," Sylvia scolded Samuel. "You are coming to the dinner. You're a part of Frakingham House now and as such, you'll be involved in all social occasions."

"Are your lives here a whirlwind of events?" he asked.

"We do our best to fulfill our responsibility as the pre-eminent house in the area."

I rolled my eyes at Samuel over Sylvia's head. He winked at me and seemed to be trying not to laugh. Frakingham may be the most established estate in the area, but social occasions were rare. We hardly even went into the village and had not entertained guests in the weeks since I'd arrived. It was no wonder they called the place Freak House behind our backs. We'd not given them reason to think otherwise.

Sylvia continued to pore over her list. "Jack, what do you think of Miss Appletree? I know she's got a face like a horse, but she's always nice to me, and she'd be quite used to invalids, her mother being bed-bound."

"I thought you weren't looking for a companion for your uncle," I said, trying to hold back my smile.

She flapped her hand in dismissal. "I'm not, but you never know when love will strike, and it's better that Uncle fall in love with someone suitable rather than a horrible old fishwife, for example."

I didn't think Langley capable of love, but I refrained from telling her that. She seemed quite fond of him, yet afraid of him in equal measure. It was an odd relationship. Langley's relationship with his nephew was equally strange. That's if Jack *was* his nephew. I wasn't entirely sure. I didn't think he was sure either. Langley himself may have been the only one who knew the entire truth, and he never answered any questions of that nature.

I glanced at Jack. Ordinarily he would have something to say about his cousin's matchmaking, but he was completely disinterested.

"Jack, what is it?" I asked, setting my palette down on the small table beside me. "You've been staring at the house for several minutes now. Is anything wrong?"

"I don't know."

"Are you listening to something? What can you hear?"

Sylvia stood too, her list forgotten. "Jack?" The frightened tremor in her voice had me worried. Did Jack often behave like this? I hadn't seen evidence of it thus far.

Samuel turned to look at the house as well. "All seems in order to me," he said. "Langley?"

Jack held up his hand for silence.

Predictably, Sylvia ignored the request. "Jack, you're frightening me."

"Wait here." He walked off across the lawn. Despite his command, Samuel followed, and I trailed behind with Sylvia holding my arm.

"It's as if he can hear something," Samuel said. "Is his hearing exceptionally good?"

"Unfortunately, yes," Sylvia muttered. "I gave up whispering to Uncle long ago when Jack was near."

"I thought I told you all to stay there," Jack said without turning around.

"See."

"Why should we remain behind?" I asked.

"Is there danger?" Samuel said, drawing up alongside Jack. They were of a similar height, their shoulders both broad, their backs straight. I was grateful they were on my side. I felt safe with them nearby. If another intruder were in Frakingham, Jack and Samuel would easily overpower him. Add Tommy the footman into the mix, and there was nothing to worry about.

So why did coils of dread twist in my stomach?

"I don't know," Jack said. "Which is why I want you all to

remain behind."

"Not going to happen," Samuel said lightly.

Jack stopped and glared at him. "I told you to stay back."

Samuel squared up to him. His eyes narrowed, his jaw set hard. There was none of the usual friendliness in the way he glared at Jack. He was all quiet determination and not at all afraid of Jack's temper.

"Mr. Langley, sir!" The foreman ran toward us, his hat scrunched in his hand.

"What is it, Yardley?" Jack asked, his conflict with Samuel forgotten.

Yardley bent over and fought for breath. "Come quickly," he said between gasps. "There's something strange in the dungeon."

"The dungeon?" Jack shook his head. "Frakingham House doesn't have a dungeon."

"He must mean the basement," Sylvia said.

"No, ma'am. I mean the dungeon. And forgive me, sir, but you do have one. Come with me, and I'll show you. Anyways, you need to see this with your own eyes. I don't know how to explain it."

He set off, Jack and Samuel at his heels. Sylvia and I lagged behind until I removed her fingers from my arm, picked up my skirts and ran after them.

"Hannah!" she called out. "Hannah, I don't think we should go."

I ignored her. She might be frightened of what Yardley had found, but my curiosity had gotten the better of me. I'd never been an overly curious person, which was perhaps fortunate since I lived in an attic for most of my life. It would have been frustrating to always want to discover what lay beyond the boundaries of Lord Wade's estate of Windamere if I'd been the inquisitive sort. What curiosity I possessed was indulged with books and maps, and that used to satisfy me most of the time. Until Jack Langley abducted me and brought me to Frakingham House. My newfound freedom had unleashed a deep-rooted desire to know everything I could about everything. My questions were ceaseless, much to my host's frustration, and my desire to see the world grew more and more every day. Once I learned to control the fire within me, I was going to travel the world.

We rounded the side of the house and stopped at a narrow trench running beside the wall. It was deep, deeper than the house's foundations, and looked like a gash slicing through flesh with the thick timber beams used as reinforcement resembling the bone structure holding the body together.

The head of one of the workmen popped out of the trench. His eyes were huge clean circles amid his dirty face. "It's getting bigger," he announced and disappeared again.

"What's getting bigger?" I asked.

Sylvia finally caught up to us. She was puffing hard, and her hat sat askew on her head. "Why is there a big hole beside the house?" she asked.

"Yardley was worried the repairs were damaging the foundations at this end," Jack said. "He dug the trench so he could reinforce them."

Sylvia put a hand to her breast. "Is it quite safe? Should we evacuate?"

"The foundations are strong now, ma'am," Yardley said. "Stronger than they've ever been. There's no basement in this part of the house, so we were able to get in easy enough. But my men discovered something just now as they were preparing to backfill."

"A dungeon," Samuel said on a breath. "You didn't know it was there?"

"No," Jack said. "There was talk that the previous house on this site had one."

Sylvia, Jack and I exchanged glances. They'd told me the stories of the children that had been kept in the dungeon by their father many years ago in the grand manor that used to occupy this site. I'd not really believed them. Tales from centuries past had a way of growing out of control and becoming distorted by each storyteller along the way. None of us had taken them seriously. But that was before we knew there was a dungeon beneath Frakingham. How much more of the stories had been real?

The hairs on the back of my neck rose, and I was happy to let Sylvia wrap her fingers around my arm and hold tight. It was a comfort, of sorts.

"This house couldn't have been built on the foundations of the old one," Yardley said. "The dungeon isn't under the house." He stomped on the ground. "It's here. We discovered it when a clump of soil fell away from the trench wall."

We all looked down. "Under our feet?" I asked.

"Yes, ma'am. It appears to run the same way as the current house, but we won't know for sure unless we go in."

"You haven't been in yet?" Samuel asked.

"We only just stumbled upon it this morning, sir. When the soil gave way, it revealed a stone wall and some rotted wood which must have once been the door. The doorway is now filled up with earth. My men dug a hole through it to look inside and realized it was another room. It was empty except for some rubble in the corner and chains attached to the walls."

"Chains!" Sylvia squeaked.

"That's why we think it's a dungeon," Yardley said. "It looks old too. The walls are stone, not brick, and thick. I'd wager it's medieval and probably been closed up since then too. It stinks like rotted meat."

"I wonder why it smells that bad," I said.

Yardley shrugged.

"So what's happened now?" Jack asked. "Before...I thought I heard something."

Yardley's mutton chop whiskers twitched. "Heard what, sir?"

Jack's gaze shifted between all of us, then he shrugged. "If no one else heard it, I must have been mistaken."

Nobody questioned him, and all seemed satisfied that he did indeed make a mistake. Except me. Jack didn't make mistakes. If he thought he'd heard something, then he had. I tried to catch his attention, but he was looking into the trench, not at me. I was close enough that I could reach out and touch his hand, but I didn't dare. Ever since we'd touched somewhat passionately in the old abbey ruins, we'd had to avoid contact of that nature. Otherwise the fire within us would be stoked, and we'd burn up from the inside. I hated it. We both did.

"So why have you called us here?" Samuel asked the foreman. "Why not simply board it up and backfill the trench?"

"Because the hole we made in the doorway…" He cleared his throat and stretched his neck out of his collar. He looked worried, something that I'd not expected to see on the weathered face of the burly, no-nonsense foreman. "It sounds odd, but the hole is getting larger of its own accord."

Jack shrugged. "Perhaps it's just caving into the cavity beyond."

"It's caving in all right, but into the trench, not into the dungeon."

As if someone were pushing out the soil from the inside.

Sylvia's hand clutched mine so hard my fingers turned numb. "Ghosts," she whispered, a tremor rippling her voice.

"Perhaps you should take the ladies inside, Gladstone," Jack said.

Samuel huffed out a derisive laugh and didn't move.

I extricated myself from Sylvia and crossed my arms. "I'm not going anywhere except down there."

"Hannah!" Sylvia cried. "You can't."

"Why not? The men are."

"Yes, but we're ladies."

I snorted. "I'm not. My parents were servants, remember?"

"Come with me, sirs," Yardley said to Jack and Samuel. He climbed down the ladder into the trench.

Jack shook his head at me and sighed. I took that as resignation and smiled back. His lips tilted up at the corners, a sure sign that he wasn't in the least angry that I was flouting his orders. "I'm sure there's a perfectly rational explanation."

He peered over the side then jumped down, avoiding the ladder altogether. Samuel did the same. It was too far for me. I gathered up my skirts and put my foot on the top rung.

"Hannah, have you gone mad?" Sylvia cried.

"Quite possibly. Being kept prisoner in an attic can do strange things to one's mind." I looked cross-eyed at her.

She groaned. "For goodness sakes, be serious. There's nothing amusing in what happened to you, and there's nothing to be gained by going down there. Let Jack and Samuel report back to us later."

I didn't know where to start with that, so I simply ignored her and kept climbing down. As my face grew level with the ground, I had the satisfaction of witnessing her stomping her booted foot.

"Hannah, I think you should listen to Sylvia," Samuel said from below.

"Save your voice, Gladstone," said Jack. "She'll do as she pleases so you might as well help her."

If Samuel thought it odd that Jack wasn't helping me himself, he didn't say and I couldn't see his expression, backing down the ladder as I was. It may not be the time for passion, but Jack's determination to keep from touching me was testament to the fact he knew desire could flare with the barest brush of skin against skin.

Samuel took my elbow and steered me to the trench floor. I thanked him and risked a glance at Jack. His gaze was fixed on Samuel's hand, still holding me. He blinked slowly and looked away.

"Are you safely down?" Sylvia called out from above.

"Yes. Care to join us?" I teased.

"No thank you. I'm going inside where it's warm, and there's no threat of the house falling on my head."

"The house won't fall on us, ma'am," Yardley said. "We're not going under it." He pointed to the wall of the trench away from the house where some large stones had indeed been revealed. A workman stood there, watching a hole the size of a fist at about waist height.

Soil trickled from the edges of the hole down the earthen wall to the trench floor. A little pile of loose dirt formed a pyramid there.

"We'd made the hole about so big," said Yardley, indicating it had come up to his chest. "After we looked inside, we filled it up again. Then this started happening just a short time ago."

Jack bent down as more soil was pushed out. He cocked his head to the side, listening.

Then he jumped back and stared at the hole. I'd never seen him look so alarmed before. It was most unlike him.

"Jack?" I asked. "What is it?"

He frowned. "You didn't hear it?"

I shook my head. Samuel and Yardley did too.

The workman who'd been squatting nearby stood. Another two builders working further along the trench put down their spades. They looked to each other, their eyes wide, frightened.

"Freak House," one of them whispered.

"I'll have none of that talk," Yardley growled. He pointed a stubby finger at each of them. "You're being paid well to not worry about idle gossip."

From the looks on the men's faces, I suspected they no longer thought they were being paid enough.

The sudden shift in their focus told me something was happening with the hole. Then the man beside me gasped loudly. I turned to see the hole had gotten much bigger. It stretched from my waist to my shoulder and kept growing.

Someone grabbed my wrist and jerked me back. Jack, I realized, somewhat startled. There were no sparks between us, no heat. We only grew hot when we touched with desire, and there was nothing romantic in the way he pinned me into his side.

"Bloody hell," he muttered. "What's that?"

"What's what?" I asked.

He blinked. "You can't see it?"

I stared hard at the hole. "No."

"What can you see?" Samuel asked quietly. He normally had a deep, melodic voice, the voice of a hypnotist, but there was nothing melodious about it now. It was edged with worry.

"Can't any of you see it?" Jack asked.

"All I see is an empty void," Samuel said. "But I don't doubt that you can see something more."

I had no time to contemplate what he meant. Jack suddenly pushed me behind him. My bustle bumped the damp earthen wall, and I couldn't see the hole anymore, only Jack's back. His breathing seemed to stop. His hands spread out to either side, protecting me.

"What is it?" I whispered.

"What can you see?" Samuel murmured, edging away from the hole.

Jack half shook his head, but said nothing. Tension gripped his shoulders. The veins in his neck strained.

And then I smelled it. Rotting meat, just like the foreman had described. I screwed up my nose and turned my face away, but the scent enveloped us entirely, filling up the trench. Someone gagged. It wasn't Jack. He hardly moved and didn't make a sound. He was entirely focused on that hole.

"Jack," I said, "what did you hear when we were on the lawn?"

"A high-pitched voice," he said without taking his eyes off the hole.

"What did it say?"

It was a moment before he spoke again, and when he did, his voice was calm, in control. "'Let me out.'"

"Oh my God."

"Then it said 'I'm going to kill you.'"

CHAPTER 2

"Get back!" Jack ordered Yardley and the workman. "Get away from the hole!"

Yardley flattened himself against the trench wall beside me. I managed to peer past Jack, but saw nothing. What could *he* see? And why couldn't the rest of us see it?

What in God's name was in the hole?

Fear gripped my insides and squeezed. I'd been terrified when Reuben Tate had tried to kill my friends and started a fire in his laboratory, but this was different. This was the fear of the unknown. I had no idea what was happening, or how that hole was getting bigger.

"Up the ladder, Hannah!" Jack shouted. "Now!"

"But—"

"Do it!" He shoved me toward the ladder. "Take her, Gladstone, and don't argue."

Samuel hustled me ahead of him. "Go, Hannah!"

"Jack!" I screamed, even though I didn't know why. All I knew was that the most self-assured man I knew looked very worried. "Please come with us."

He held up his fingers and flames danced on the tips. Yardley shrank back, stumbling over his feet in his hurry to get away. The two far workmen stared at the flames, terror widening their eyes. The other one closest to the hole wasn't looking at Jack, but at the void, an expression of child-like curiosity on his face. He scrabbled at the edges, helping to widen it. Helping whatever was beyond the wall to get out.

Samuel swore softly. "You two have a lot to tell me when this is over." He pushed me up the ladder.

My skirts got in the way, and I scooped them up in one hand and used the other to climb. Samuel was right behind me. Climbing a ladder ahead of a man was a terribly unladylike thing to do, but propriety was not my top priority.

I was almost at the highest rung when I felt Samuel's hand on my rear. He gave one almighty shove and I sailed over the edge of the trench. I fell on my hands and knees on the muddy ground.

Before I could get up, Samuel grabbed me by the arms and hauled me to my feet. I looked around just in time to see Yardley and two of the workmen piling out of the trench.

"Get out!" Jack shouted.

"Not yet," the second worker said. "Let me just—"

"Run!"

Jack probably meant the worker, but Yardley and his other men took it as a sign to sprint off around the side of the house.

"Come on," Samuel said, holding my hand. "Let's go."

"But…Jack!"

"After what I saw him do without matches, I think he'll be fine."

I wasn't so confident, but I knew Jack was better suited to face whatever came out of that hole than any of us.

A whoosh of air blasted from the trench and a shimmer of heat rose up. A high-pitched scream followed. It didn't sound human.

"*Jack!*" I tried to pull away from Samuel, but he held me too tightly.

Another scream stopped my heart dead in my chest. This time it *was* human.

Oh God.

I jerked and fought to free myself, but Samuel was too strong. He spoke soothing words in my ear, but I couldn't hear them above the screaming and the blood pounding in my head. "We have to help!"

Samuel didn't let go, despite my struggles. He'd stopped talking though, as if he knew he wasn't getting through to me. The screams kept coming.

Another whoosh of fire and heat blew out of the trench. Immediately the screams changed. The human one stopped abruptly, and the other high-pitched one took over.

I saw it then. A mere disturbance of the air at the lip of the trench, like a ripple of invisible waves. It was coming toward us.

Samuel saw it too. He dove off to the side, dragging me with him. We landed awkwardly, but the mud and grass cushioned our fall.

I looked up as a strong breeze swept past. It ruffled my hair, warmed my skin. At this time of year, any breeze should have been cold. Samuel threw a protective arm over my head, but the disturbance had already gone.

"Jack!" I shouted, shoving Samuel away.

We approached the trench cautiously, our hands linked for comfort. Nobody emerged. A single sob bubbled up from my chest and lodged in my throat. What had happened to him?

I dared not peer over the edge. I didn't want to see. Those screams…

A hand clutched the top rung of the ladder. Clean hands with reddened fingers.

I raced to the trench and lay down on my stomach. I didn't care about dirtying my clothes. I grasped Jack's hands, then his forearms and finally his face as he emerged.

I kissed him hard on the lips. All of my relief at seeing him alive and unharmed poured out of me through that kiss. I held his face, caressed his hair, and cried pathetically.

Until the heat inside became too much. Jack pulled away first with a groan. His face was flushed and sweat dotted his hairline. I'd forgotten that he must already have been hot from using his fire. Heat also swirled within me and raced along my veins. It wasn't unbearable, but it was decidedly uncomfortable.

Samuel's boots appeared beside me. He helped me to stand and offered his hand to Jack. Jack took it and emerged fully from the trench. He glanced around while Samuel looked down.

"Poor man," Samuel muttered. "No, Hannah," he said when I went to peek. He steered me away from the trench. "Don't look."

My stomach rolled anyway. My imagination was vivid enough to visualize all the horrible things that could have happened to the remaining workman.

Jack looked past us toward the woods. "Take her into the house and lock the doors."

"Why?" I asked. "Jack, what...what was in the dungeon?"

He fixed his gaze on me, and I shivered. The horror of what he'd just witnessed was reflected in his eyes. It chilled me to the bone, and I did not usually feel cold. "It wasn't like anything I've ever seen before."

"Describe it."

He shook his head and glanced over his shoulder at the trench. "Take her, Gladstone. Don't let anyone out."

I would have pressed him for details, but he did not look in a mood to give any. "What about you?" I asked. "Aren't you coming?"

"It needs to be stopped."

"You can't do it! Not on your own. Go for the police. Tell them—"

"What? That a creature that no one but me could see killed a man after it escaped from our hidden dungeon? They won't believe me." He glanced at the woods again. "They're not equipped to catch that thing anyway."

"Neither are you!" I was crying and shaking. All I wanted to do was hold him in my arms and breathe in his scent, but I couldn't. Our bodies forbade such touches. I couldn't even talk some sense into him. He had such a look of determination that I knew nothing I could say would convince him to come with me.

"Hannah," he murmured, caressing my hair near my face. It was the closest we could be at such moments without feeling like we'd combust. "Hannah, go inside. I'll be fine. You know I will."

I bit my cheek to hold back the tears. They welled anyway. "I know nothing of the sort."

He almost smiled at that. "Don't make me order Samuel to drag you into the house. It would be very unbecoming. The servants will talk."

I clicked my tongue. "You are so stubborn, Jack Langley."

"Said the queen of stubbornness."

"I won't be dragging her anywhere," Samuel cut in. "I'm coming with you."

"No," Jack said.

"Hannah's right. You can't do this alone."

"I have to. *You* can't see it. I can."

"And why is that?"

Jack shook his head. "I don't know. All I know is you'll be more of a liability than an asset. My fire protected me and scared it away, but next time it may not be frightened off so easily. If it catches you…" He swallowed hard and glanced at the trench. "When it came out, it went straight for the worker. I tried a small fire in the hope he wouldn't be too harmed, but it wasn't enough to stop the creature…devouring him."

I pressed my hand over my mouth as bile rose to my throat. Devouring?

"When it finished, it came at me. I threw the most powerful fireball I could, and it fled. So you see, I can't protect both myself and you. Stay in the house, Gladstone. Keep everyone calm. I'll be back soon."

Samuel offered me his arm and I took it. My heart thumped against my ribs. This was madness. Our pleasant morning had been shattered, a man was dead, and Jack was about to chase the murdering creature into the woods. I felt like Alice walking through the looking glass into another, stranger world.

"Be careful," I said, rather pathetically.

"Aren't I always?"

I watched him go. He turned back when he reached the edge of the woods and pointed at the house. Samuel made me walk off with him.

"I don't know how I'll keep calm while we wait," I said.

"I do. You can tell me how Langley made fire dance across his fingers, and why you felt hot just now. I think my hand got singed as I assisted you to stand."

All the workmen had disappeared from the scaffolding, no doubt leaving when they saw their colleagues running away. Once inside, we locked the door, and I went straight to the service area and asked Mrs. Moore the housekeeper and Tommy the footman to join me in the small room she used as her office.

"Is this to do with the shouting?" Mrs. Moore asked. "Maud came to me and said she heard the builders when she was down that end of the house."

I closed my eyes. The screams still rang in my ears and sent fresh shivers through me. The phrase blood-curdling came to mind, but it didn't capture the sheer terror threaded through that scream, or my visceral reaction to it.

"There's been a wild dog attack on one of the builders," I said. "Mr. Jack Langley is looking for the animal to…ensure it doesn't happen again."

"A wild dog?" Tommy said, frowning. "What sort of dog?"

I gave my head a slight shake to curb his questions. Tommy was an old friend of Jack's. He knew all about our fire starting and as such would probably accept that sometimes inexplicable things happened. Mrs. Moore and the other servants were simple villagers. I didn't want to send them into hysterics by telling them an invisible creature ate a man.

Both orphans, Jack and Tommy had grown up on the streets of London together, until August Langley had found his nephew and brought him to Frakingham House. Then aged fourteen, they would not be separated, so Tommy was given a position as footman.

He'd helped us in our fight against Reuben Tate two weeks earlier, and because of that, the barrier of social class had slipped a little, but only at rare moments. Most of the time, Tommy performed his duty with a footman's blank stare and perfect manners. This was not one of those times. His eyes widened slightly and he acknowledged my reticence with a small nod.

Mrs. Moore's wrinkles scooped together into a frown. "Is the builder all right? Does he need medical assistance?"

I lowered my head and heard her gasp of horrified understanding. "Don't frighten the other servants," I told her. "But don't let them out either. Not until Mr. Jack Langley says it's safe. Tommy, fetch Olsen from the stables. Take a weapon with you for protection. On second thoughts, take a burning piece of wood from one of the fireplaces. It doesn't seem to like fire."

He gave me another nod of understanding.

"When you return, bring tea to the parlor."

Tommy and Mrs. Moore left. I went straight to the parlor where I found Sylvia arguing with Samuel near the fireplace. Her face was pink and flushed, her fists closed at her sides as if she were holding back from pummeling the answers out of poor Samuel. He eyed her with a rather alarmed look on his face. He'd never seen Sylvia in a temper. Ordinarily she was serene and meek, perfectly content to embroider or read in the parlor by the fire, but that composure could crack under pressure. Sometimes I wondered if her dainty politeness was just a mask she'd spent years perfecting and a formidable persona lurked beneath.

"Tell me!" she ordered Samuel.

"Sylvia," I said. "Come and sit down until the others

arrive. Where is your uncle?"

"He's on his way. I know something is terribly wrong, Hannah. You locked all the doors and Samuel keeps looking out the window." She glanced past me to the door. "Where's Jack?"

"I'll explain in a moment. Let's wait for your uncle and Tommy."

"Tommy?" The fight left her, and she plopped down on the sofa beside me as if her legs had given way. "Where is he?"

"Fetching Olsen from the stables."

"You're terrifying me now, Hannah. Why does Olsen need to be inside the house? Was it wise for Tommy to go out at all?"

I wanted to assure her everything would be all right, that Jack, Tommy, Olsen, everybody would waltz into the parlor soon and all would be well. But I couldn't form the words. I held her hand and said nothing. It didn't help. She was a tightly coiled rope, trembling with tension.

The strained silence was broken by August Langley's arrival, wheeled in by Bollard. He took over the interrogation that Sylvia had let slide.

I held up my hand to stop him. "Wait for Tommy."

August Langley wasn't used to taking orders from others, and it showed in his pursed lips and flared nostrils. I didn't know why Langley was wheelchair-bound. I suspected it was due to an accident that had occurred when he worked with Tate in their laboratory. Both men were microbiologists, and eight years ago they sold a highly sought-after remedy for a great deal of money. Langley had bought Frakingham House with the proceeds, while Tate had squandered his portion. Langley continued to work on new drugs, assisted by Bollard, his valet. His research had been curbed of late after the fire destroyed his rooms and much of his equipment.

Bollard stood behind Langley just inside the doorway. The mute servant stared ahead as if he were oblivious to the tension in the room. But I knew he was listening and wondering. He might not talk, but he could hear perfectly well. I suspected he wasn't as indifferent as he appeared.

Fortunately Tommy arrived, putting an end to Sylvia and Langley's frustration. All eyes turned to Samuel and me. Together we told them what we'd seen and heard, and how Jack was now looking for the...thing.

Tommy was the first to speak when we finished. "So what is it?"

Langley frowned, clearly annoyed that the footman had forgotten his place. Tommy seemed not to notice.

I shook my head. "I don't know. For now, I think we should tell the servants it's a wild dog. We shouldn't alarm them."

"A wise decision," Langley said, giving a nod of approval.

"So why was Jack the only one who could see it?" Sylvia asked.

I shrugged. The question had been bothering me too, but there was simply no reasonable explanation.

Samuel cleared his throat. "Perhaps it has something to do with being able to start fires with nothing but his fingers." His eyebrows lifted pointedly at me. "Would someone like to explain that?"

We'd managed to hide our fire starting ability from him so far. It wasn't that I was ashamed of it or worried that he'd label us as freaks, but there had simply never been a good time to tell him. *'By the way, Jack and I can start fires with our minds'* didn't seem like a suitable start to dinnertime conversation.

"It's something he was born with," I said. "At least, we think he was born with it. He can't recall a time when he couldn't set things alight with a point of his fingers. I'm able to do it too, just not at will. Mine is linked to my temper. It makes life...interesting."

Samuel snorted and began to laugh. When he saw that none of us laughed too, it died on his lips. "You're serious," he said flatly.

I nodded.

"I'll try not to anger you then."

"A wise decision."

"Who else knows? The servants?"

"Nobody else," Langley said. "Tell a soul, and you won't be living here any longer, Mr. Gladstone. We don't need the extra attention."

"We have quite enough of it already," Sylvia agreed. "Some people call this place Freak House, you know."

"So I've heard. That's not because of the fire starting?"

"No. There are other freakish things to keep them satisfied." She didn't have to look at Bollard and Langley for everyone to know whom she meant. Everyone except Bollard and Langley, that is. Having a mute and a wheelchair-bound recluse living at Frakingham had been quite enough for the Harborough villagers to perpetuate the Freak House moniker.

"The stories," Langley muttered to himself. "The stories about the Frakingham children."

"Uncle?" Sylvia prompted.

I knew what he meant. Oh God, I knew. "One of the Lords Frakingham kept his children locked away," I reminded her. "You told me about him yourself."

"Good lord," Samuel murmured.

Sylvia stared at me. "Oh my! You're right. Could it be...?"

"What?" Samuel asked. "What is it?"

"One of the Lords Frakingham from centuries past is rumored to have kept his deformed children locked away," I said. "In the *dungeon*."

His lips formed a full O.

"A dungeon we didn't know existed until today."

Langley wheeled himself into our tight circle, leaving Bollard behind near the door. "The creature Jack saw...it may be the ghost of one of those children. Spirits that can't or won't cross over to the Otherworld remain in this realm."

"Now you're telling me spirits are real too?" Samuel scoffed. "Fire starting I can believe, almost, but ghosts are purely in the realm of fantasy."

"You think that because you can't see them," Langley said.

"Can you?"

"No, but others can."

Samuel snorted. "I thought you were a man of science and reason, Mr. Langley."

"And I thought *you* were a natural hypnotist born with that ability, Samuel," I said. "Can you explain *that*?" It wasn't often I felt compelled to defend August Langley. Indeed, make that *never*. But Samuel was being particularly obstinate in this case, and it wasn't fair to accuse Langley of setting aside his scientific reasoning. It was because he was a scientist that he believed in the paranormal. He'd seen evidence of it enough through Jack's fire starting.

"It would seem I'm out-witted," Samuel said with a slight bow to me. "I'll concede that ghosts may indeed exist, but I don't understand why Jack could see it and we couldn't."

"Perhaps he's a spirit medium," Sylvia said. "Like that Mrs. Beaufort."

"Perhaps," I said, although I thought it unlikely since he'd never seen a ghost until now.

"Once again," Samuel said with barely contained patience, "I am in the dark. Who is Mrs. Beaufort?"

"A spirit medium of course," Sylvia said with a roll of her eyes. "One of the few legitimate ones. Uncle August met her years ago, didn't you, Uncle?"

Langley nodded. "She is also the patroness of a school for orphans in London."

"*And* married to a viscount's heir," Sylvia added with a sigh. "What a thrilling life."

"I don't think I'd want to be able to see ghosts," Tommy said. He'd been standing so quietly off to the side that I'd almost forgotten he was there. I felt a little guilty. I'd not thought the servants would ever become invisible to me, but it seemed I was little better than Langley and Sylvia in that regard. Samuel and Jack always seemed aware when a servant was in the room and spoke to them like they were real people, but Sylvia and her uncle treated the servants as if they were a piece of furniture, functional but not worthy of much attention. I didn't want to become like them.

"Nor I," I said. "It's quite enough to be able to start fires, thank you. I'm sure Jack would agree if he were here."

Samuel went to stand by the window. There was still no sign of Jack. I didn't want to think about him out there. Didn't want to think about how he was going to find that…thing, and if he did, what he'd do. Nor did I want to think about the dead body in the trench. We still had to notify the police, the man's family...oh God.

"You need a name for it," Sylvia declared suddenly.

"Pardon?" I asked.

"A name. For the fire starting. Someone who sees ghosts is called a medium, someone who sees the future is known as a seer, so what should we call you and Jack? We need a word that rolls off the tongue."

"What's wrong with fire starter?" I asked.

"It sounds awkward and consists of two words. One would be better." Her hands twisted in her lap, over and over. I knew her well enough to know that she was worried about Jack but determined not to show it. If there was one thing she would never admit, it was that she cared for her cousin. They may disagree often and tease each other mercilessly, but they were family.

"Sylvia, you're being ridiculous," Langley scolded. "This is not the time to think of such frivolities."

I certainly didn't agree with him about that. Now was exactly the time. We all needed a distraction from the painful wait for Jack to return. "Does anyone know the Latin word for fire?"

"Ignis," Samuel said. "Or there's flamma meaning flame and inflammo is torch."

"Torch isn't quite right, but I like flamma," said Sylvia. "What about autoflamma? Self-flaming."

I screwed up my nose. "It doesn't have the right ring to

it."

"And you're mixing Greek and Latin," Samuel said.

There was a knock on the front door of the house. "Jack!" Sylvia cried, leaping off the settee, our exercise in linguistics forgotten.

We followed her out to the entrance hall, and Tommy opened the door. He was the first to slap Jack on the back, Samuel the second. Sylvia hugged him, and Langley gripped his forearm.

I hung back. My heart had swelled to twice its size and tears blurred my vision. I was so grateful to see him again, but I couldn't touch him like the others. The way I felt at that moment, seeing him with windswept hair and flushed skin but completely unharmed, I would have combusted immediately. As it was, I felt hot enough just looking at him. Hot and suddenly exhausted. The wait had been excruciating on my nerves.

Jack must have known why I kept my distance. He offered a small but troubled smile and said, "Hello, Hannah. Are you all right?"

I laughed. "You're asking *me* if I'm all right?"

"Are you?"

"No!" I said still smiling stupidly through tears of relief. "I've been absolutely terrified waiting for you. We all have."

"Well?" Langley said, gruff. "Has it gone?"

Jack shook his head.

"You mean it's still out there?" Sylvia cried.

Jack put his arm around her shoulders. "You'll be safe here."

"But we'll be prisoners in the house."

"Uncle never goes out and you hardly do either in winter," Jack said. "The rest of the household…" He looked at me. "The rest of us will have to find something to occupy ourselves until it's caught."

"Tell us about it," Langley said. "What was it?"

"Not out here," I said. Mrs. Moore or one of the servants could come at any moment, and we couldn't risk them overhearing. "Come into the parlor. Tommy, a fresh pot of tea please."

"I need something stronger than tea," Jack said.

Tommy disappeared down the corridor that led to the service area. We made our way back to the parlor.

"Well?" Langley blurted out before we were completely settled once more.

Jack shook his head and shrugged. "I don't know. I've never seen anything like it."

"Describe it."

Jack looked at Sylvia and me sitting side by side on the settee. "Not in front of the ladies."

"We're not so delicate that we can't hear the details," I said.

Sylvia pressed a hand to her stomach. "Speak for yourself." She did not leave, however. Perhaps, like me, she felt compelled to hear more despite feeling sick.

Tommy arrived with glasses and two bottles on a silver tray. He set the tray down and filled two of the glasses. He handed one to Jack and the other to Samuel. Langley declined.

"Sherry?" he asked Sylvia and me. We both nodded and accepted a glass.

"It was human," Jack said, holding his tumbler between the fingertips of both hands. "Yet not."

"That doesn't make sense," Sylvia said.

"In what way was it human?" Samuel asked. "It had arms, legs and a head?"

"You could be describing an animal," I said.

"Animal is a more fitting description than human." Jack sipped thoughtfully. "It stood upright, however. It was large. Larger than me, but hunched over. It had claws and jagged teeth, and fur all over its body."

"So we weren't too wrong when we told the servants it was a wild dog," I muttered.

Sylvia swallowed her entire glass of sherry and held it out for a refill. Tommy obliged.

"Did it have a canine face?" Samuel asked.

Jack shook his head. "Not particularly. Its ears were pointed but small, its nose longer and wider than anything I've ever seen, but I wouldn't call it a muzzle. The eyes were yellow. When it looked at me..." He drained the glass. "When it looked at me, I thought I saw fear in those eyes. Fear and desperation. Very human emotions. But then something changed. It was like something else took over entirely, and any humanity it displayed vanished. The only emotion I recognized was hunger. It wanted to kill."

"If it hadn't been for your fire," I said, quietly, "it may have killed you."

"Instead, it went for the builder." He shook his head and looked down at his glass. "Why didn't he leave when the others did?"

"Why didn't you?"

Samuel, Sylvia and I finished our drinks in unison. The sherry burned my throat as it went down. It didn't calm my frayed nerves like I'd hoped.

"Hannah told us it spoke to you," Langley said.

Jack nodded. "I don't know if it spoke to me specifically, but I seemed to be the only one who could hear the screams and understand it."

"It spoke English?"

"Yes."

"How strange," Samuel muttered.

"Did you recognize the voice?" Langley asked.

We all turned to stare at him. "Why would he recognize the voice?" I said cautiously. The conversation had taken an even more disturbing turn.

"Uncle?" Sylvia said when he didn't answer me.

"Did you recognize it?" Langley asked again.

Jack stretched out his long legs and sat back in the chair. "Not as such, but it was high-pitched and childish."

"Oh my God," Sylvia whispered. "What *was* it?"

We all looked to Langley. "I believe that you encountered a demon," he said. "One that has taken on the souls of the long-dead Frakingham children."

CHAPTER 3

I stared at Langley, my mouth ajar. The brief but charged silence was punctured by Samuel's snort of derision.

"There's no such thing as demons," he said. "I don't think you ought to frighten the ladies like that, Langley."

Sylvia did indeed look frightened. Her entire body trembled, and her eyes were so wide that I thought she might strain a nerve.

"Didn't we already establish the existence of the supernatural?" I asked. "I thought you'd come to terms with it, Samuel."

"Ghosts I can accept." He wiggled his fingers. "Even your fire I will acknowledge is not out of the realms of possibility, as are my hypnotic abilities. But you're asking me to believe in an entity that is neither human nor animal, but something else entirely. If demons exist, why aren't we overrun by them? That thing and its ilk would be quite capable of obliterating entire villages."

The thought of several of those things going on a rampage sickened me even more. I tended to agree with his logic. "I see your point. Surely we'd be aware of them if they existed."

"Have you never wondered about unexplained phenomena?" Jack asked. "The disappearance of people without a trace, the occasional sightings of strange creatures in the woods?" He nodded at the window. "The horrible death of a man by wild dogs when there are no wild dogs in the area."

Sylvia folded her arms and hugged herself. "I must say, I like to think Hannah and Samuel are right."

"That would involve denying what I saw today," Jack said. "Hannah and Samuel didn't see it."

"In that case, I shall remain in denial," Sylvia said.

I rubbed my forehead. It ached, and I still felt sick to my stomach. That poor man's screams would never leave me.

"Perhaps it's wise to keep an open mind," Samuel said. "I'll concede that I don't have an answer for everything."

Jack gave a grudging laugh.

"What should we do now?" Samuel went on. "If it is demonic, how do we capture it?"

"The first thing we must do is alert the authorities," Langley said. "Jack, ride into the village and tell the police about the death. We'll keep to the wild dog story. Claiming otherwise would be counter-productive. In my experience any suggestion of the supernatural is met with ridicule, denial and occasionally admission to an asylum."

"Oh, thank goodness," Sylvia said. "I was worried you would try to convince the police of the existence of demons. We're quite ostracized enough as it is and with the dinner party at such a crucial stage of planning, the mere whiff of something freakish here would be social suicide."

"A man has just died, Syl," Jack said tightly. "The dinner party is the least of our concerns."

Sylvia seemed to deflate, as if his sharp glare had pricked her.

"What happens after the authorities have been told?" I asked. "They won't catch it, so what should we do?"

"We must find someone who knows more than we do about demons," Langley said.

"Who?"

"I'm not sure, but I can ask Mr. and Mrs. Beaufort."

"Isn't she a spirit medium?" Jack said. "What do they know about demons?"

"They have first-hand knowledge." He lifted his hand to stem our questions. "I'm retiring to my rooms to continue with my work. Hannah, you look somewhat pale. Perhaps you ought to rest until dinner."

I was taken aback by his observation. Unless he was asking me something specific about my training with Jack, he usually ignored me. I wasn't used to him noticing my health. "I'm quite all right. Thank you."

"He's right," Jack said, crouching at my feet. "The events of today seem to have taken their toll on you. Or is it something else? Are you worried about the trial?"

The pending trial of Reuben Tate was certainly on my mind, but it didn't keep me awake at night. Whenever I thought about him in prison, the overwhelming emotion was one of relief. The madman had tried to kill my friends and abduct me in order to use me in his experiments. I was glad he was locked away.

"It's not that," I assured him.

"There'll be no training for a few days," he said. "We don't seem to be making progress anyway."

"That's precisely why she should continue," Langley said. "She needs to take control of her ability. The sooner the better." His vehemence alarmed me. Why was he so adamant?

"She's tired, August," Jack said. "Let her rest."

"I am," Langley growled. "Did I not just order her to her room?"

Order me? I thought it was a suggestion, a kindness even. I should have known August Langley was quite without that commodity.

"Let me escort you," Jack said quietly. He offered a smile, but not his hand. That would have been foolish.

"No." Langley rolled himself a few paces forward until

he'd wedged himself between us. "Samuel will do it."

Samuel frowned. "Why?" He caught sight of Langley's narrowed glare and muttered, "Of course. Hannah, would you care to take my arm?"

Jack scowled first at Samuel then at Langley. He stormed out of the parlor ahead of us. Samuel and I found him waiting in the corridor near my bedroom door. I went to him and put my hand on the doorknob. He leaned against the wall, very close.

"Get some rest, Hannah." He folded his arms and tucked his hands away as if he were smothering them. Was he hot just being near me? I certainly felt warmer from head to toe. His presence had a profound effect.

"Are you going to Harborough now?" I asked, pulling away from Samuel, but not venturing any closer to Jack.

"I'll be back in an hour."

"Be careful."

The corner of his mouth lifted. "Always."

He didn't leave until I was inside. I heard him and Samuel walking back along the corridor together. "I didn't have a choice," Samuel said.

"There is always a choice," Jack said. "Even with him."

***

By the time I woke up an hour later, Jack had returned with the police, a doctor and undertaker. The doctor and undertaker took the remains of the body away in their cart while the police searched the woods. They were gone until dusk, but of course found no traces of a wild dog. Jack itched to join them, but they forbade it. He did encourage them to take burning torches to ward off the animal. Some listened. Others armed themselves with guns. All returned unharmed, thank God.

"They'll look again in the morning," Jack said when he returned to the parlor after speaking to the detective inspector.

Samuel set down the notebook he'd been reading. "Hopefully it's long gone."

"To terrorize elsewhere?" I shook my head. "Let's hope not."

We moved into the dining room where Tommy served us. As usual, Langley ate in his rooms, attended by Bollard. It was a bleak affair with the events of the day hanging heavily over us.

"We ought to pay for the builder's funeral at the very least," Sylvia said.

Jack agreed. "I'll speak to August after dinner. We should set up a fund for the widow."

I pushed my food around my plate as the others discussed arrangements. It kept their fear away, I suppose, but I couldn't join in. I couldn't stop thinking about what Langley had said—that the invisible creature had been a demon, and it had consumed the souls of the poor Frakingham children.

"What do we know of the dungeon and its...occupants?" I asked during a lull in their conversation.

"Oh, Hannah, do we *have* to talk about it?" Sylvia said on a sigh. "I suppose we do," she added before I could respond.

"We know nothing about demons." I glanced at each of my fellow diners as well as Tommy, standing by the sideboard. "Until we hear from Mr. and Mrs. Beaufort, we ought to concentrate on what we do know, and that is the Frakingham estate and history."

"Freak House," Sylvia muttered. "I hate this place."

"Actually, I like it," I said.

She screwed up her pretty nose. "It's so gloomy."

"It's better than being locked away in the attic at Windamere."

She looked thoughtful for a moment. "Of course it is. I'm sorry, Hannah"

I glanced at Samuel. Although we'd told him about my past at Lord Wade's house, I still felt awkward that he knew the entire story. I didn't want him to think of me as a closeted innocent. I might be in awe of the new things I saw and heard every day since Jack had abducted me and brought me to Frakingham, but I *was* educated and, I liked to think, quite normal. If one didn't take the fire starting into account, and the fact that I was a cured narcoleptic.

"Are there any records?" I asked.

"What sort of records?" Jack said.

"Letters or diaries would be ideal, but it was so long ago that those things are probably lost, if they ever existed. If we could find some records of the children's births, that would be a good place to start. At least then we'll have names."

"I'm not sure what finding any of that would achieve," Sylvia muttered.

"Perhaps nothing, but it has to be better than waiting for Mr. and Mrs. Beaufort to respond. Or would you rather think up names for Jack's and my talent?"

"There's no need for sarcasm, Hannah. I'm capable of doing both."

Tommy cleared his throat. "Mrs. Moore may be aware of any personal documents that have been stored away."

"Excellent," said Samuel. "And Langley may know what was included with the purchase of the house."

Both Tommy and Samuel seemed quite energized by the prospect of seeking out historical documents, but Jack did not. He eyed me carefully. "It may involve looking through the attic," he said quietly. He sat on Sylvia's other side, and she sat next to me, cutting her meat as if she'd not heard his pained tone or seen him wince.

"Honestly, Jack, did you have to mention attics at all?" she said.

I looked past her to Jack and smiled my gratitude. "It's kind of you to worry about me, but I'm not claustrophobic. I'll look forward to seeing what's up there. Shall we begin tomorrow morning?"

"I'll look forward to it," he said.

"I'll wear my oldest dress," Sylvia declared. "I wouldn't want to get dust over anything nice."

***

The police widened their search for the "wild dog" while

we began our search through the Frakingham attic for anything that might be linked to the earl who'd locked his children away. I felt a twinge of apprehension as I followed Jack into the dark room with the high vaulted ceilings on the undamaged southern side of the house, but it was soon extinguished. The attic was nothing like the rooms in which I had lived at Windamere Manor. While those walls had been covered with woolen rugs to prevent me setting them alight, they were at least bright and airy. The Frakingham attic was dimly lit and smelled as if it hadn't been opened up in years. It was crowded with chests and trunks, some of them spilling their contents onto the floor, as well as furniture and an alarming number of preserved dead animals.

"I think the previous owner enjoyed hunting," Samuel said, testing the sharpness of a set of antlers with his finger.

Sylvia held her lamp up to a stuffed badger's body perched atop a table. "Thank goodness Uncle saw fit to remove all of these from downstairs."

"And put up your pictures instead," Jack teased. "Lucky us."

Sylvia poked her tongue out at him.

Samuel ran his finger along an old brass lamp base. It came away filthy. "It seems you ladies had the right idea to wear old clothing. I'm afraid we're all going to leave covered in dust."

"Mrs. Moore apologizes for not cleaning up here for some time," Jack said. "I told her not to worry. The areas we do frequent are quite enough for her."

Sylvia sneezed. "Still, it appears as if she hasn't been up here since we moved in. There are cobwebs over everything."

I opened the curtains covering one of the three arched windows, throwing light into the room. Sylvia extinguished her lamp and settled on her knees in front of a carved wooden box. Jack found a chest of drawers to search through, and Samuel picked up a crate full of books. I opened the other curtains, but stopped as I parted the third.

The air left my body in a rush.

Jack was at my side in an instant. "What is it, Hannah?"

I pointed out the window. Down below on the gravel drive, Tommy held open the door of a grand carriage. I recognized the escutcheon emblazoned on the side, and the man who emerged was someone I'd seen only rarely but knew even from a distance.

Lord Wade.

"What the bloody hell does he want?" Jack snarled.

Sylvia and Samuel crowded about me. Sylvia's arm snaked around my waist. "Are you all right, Hannah? Do you need to sit down?" Sometimes she could be the sweetest creature in the world.

"I'd like to go downstairs and see what he wants," I said.

All three of them exchanged glances. "I don't know if that's a good idea," Sylvia hedged. "Let Uncle speak to him."

"If Hannah wants to talk to him, then she should," Jack said. "I'm sure she has questions she'd like to ask."

That was quite the understatement. If I wrote down all the questions I had for Lord Wade, I'd have a list as high as the room.

"Will you come with me?" I asked him.

"Of course."

We made our way downstairs. I wish I'd worn something more appropriate than one of Sylvia's old dresses. He was an earl after all. It seemed a silly thing to worry about though.

I heard Lord Wade's voice before I saw him. It was big and powerful, much like the man himself, and carried to us as we approached the small parlor.

"It's been a long time, Langley," he said.

August Langley had already told me he'd known Lord Wade from their time together in the Society For Supernatural Activity. He'd also said he'd given me to Wade when I was a baby to keep me safe from Reuben Tate. Apparently he'd not known I was kept in the attic at Windamere, not until my governess, Miss Levine, had contacted him and asked him to take me back.

"What do you want, Wade?" Langley asked. His tone surprised me. There was no deference to the other man's superiority, no hint of the fact he'd once trusted Wade to take care of me. He spoke to Wade as if he'd done something reprehensible, which he had. He'd locked me away.

Apparently the tone surprised Wade too. He took a moment to answer, and when he did, he sounded less blustery. "I, uh, thought you should know that she's gone." When Langley didn't answer, he added, "The girl you brought to me eighteen years ago. She just…disappeared one day."

Jack and I had reached the door, but I put up my hand to halt him. I wanted to hear what these men had to say before we entered. It could shed some much-needed light on the subject of my past.

"Perhaps she walked away of her own accord," Langley said.

"Why would she do that?"

"How would I know what goes through the mind of a young woman? Did you treat her well?"

Wade's hesitation was telling. "I gave her everything she could possibly need, and I never raised a hand to her."

"Which is as I'd hoped. It's why I gave her to you in the first place. You're a gentleman of integrity." Sarcasm soured the words, but it was impossible to know if Wade detected it or not. He may be oblivious since he wasn't aware that Langley knew I'd been kept in the attic.

"We've heard nothing from her in the weeks since her disappearance," Lord Wade said. "No letters asking for money, not even a note to her friend to tell her she's all right. It's not like her. They were devoted to one another."

I would have challenged him over that if I didn't want to remain hidden. His daughter Violet had been involved in my kidnapping. Miss Levine may have orchestrated it with August Langley, but Vi had been an integral part of the operation. Her betrayal had shattered me. I doubt she'd ever been devoted, as he put it. I had been to her once. Not anymore.

"We ought to consider that her departure wasn't voluntary," Wade said.

"You think Tate took her?"

"Of course I think Tate took her! Why else would I be here? Listen to me, Langley, we have to find her. It's been weeks. He could have done anything by now, be anywhere. I should have contacted you earlier, but I thought...hoped ...she'd return. I've been a fool."

"Yes. You have." In a louder voice, Langley said, "You can come in now, Hannah."

I gasped and took a step back. Bollard appeared at the door. If his presence was meant to encourage me, it failed. Or perhaps he was there to catch me if I tried to run away.

"It's all right, Hannah," Jack said. "I'll be with you."

We might not be able to touch intimately, but his presence was enough to fortify my nerves. I gave him a smile of thanks and walked into the parlor. Bollard blocked the doorway as soon as I passed him.

"Not you, Jack," Langley said.

"Bollocks," Jack said and muscled his way through. It had to be said that Bollard stepped aside quite quickly, earning a scowl from Langley.

Lord Wade rose out of his chair. "Hannah! You're safe, thank God."

I'd only seen him face to face a few times in all the years I was relegated to the attic. I'd stared at the top of his head often when he climbed into and out of his carriage far below the window, but it wasn't the same. He was as tall as I remembered and solid across the chest, but the stoop of his shoulders was new. The lines across his forehead and around his eyes also seemed deeper than before. He wasn't quite so intimidating.

"Lord Wade." I curtseyed with my head bowed as Miss Levine had taught us to do.

"What are you doing here?" he blurted out.

"I had her kidnapped from Windamere," Langley said.

"You did what!"

Langley held up his hands for calm. "It's too late for outrage, Wade. You've kept her in the attic for fifteen years, and you waited three weeks before reporting her missing."

Wade sat heavily and smoothed his moustache with his thumb and forefinger. "Hannah...are you all right? Has Langley treated you well?"

"Yes, thank you. I've been free to come and go." More or less. Aside from the first few days of my stay, I'd not been a prisoner at Frakingham. Unlike at Windamere.

Wade had the decency to look sheepish. "Good," he muttered. "Good." He pushed himself out of the chair. "It seems there's nothing else for me to do here. I'll be going."

"You don't want to know why or how I was kidnapped?" I asked. "Come now, my lord, you've had a long journey. Stay and take refreshments with us. Bollard, fetch some tea, please."

Bollard didn't move. I suspected taking orders from me wasn't part of his job or in his nature.

"I don't want tea," Wade said. "As to the why and how, I'm sure Langley has his reasons." The thick, bushy brows crashed together. "Who am I to question his motives? He and Tate always had their little secrets, their mysterious research that no one was allowed to ask them about. You see, Hannah, I'm well aware that August Langley isn't someone who can be idly questioned. Not if one expects a straight answer, that is."

Langley clicked his tongue. "So cynical."

"I know you well."

"People can change over eighteen years."

"Not in my experience."

"Lord Wade," I said, cutting through their squabbling. "You may not wish to know why Mr. Langley kidnapped me, but I'd like to know some things from you. Please sit back down."

Those impressive brows rose again. "I don't like your

tone, young lady."

"I did say please."

He grunted but sat.

"Thank you." I had to be careful. I didn't want to raise his ire and discourage any answers he may be otherwise willing to give. "It was Miss Levine who contacted Mr. Langley," I said. "She and Violet wished to be rid of me."

From the shocked look on his face it was clear he didn't know. "Why?" he muttered more to himself than anyone else.

"That's what I'd like to discover."

He leaned back into the deeply cushioned chair and did not meet my gaze for some time. When he did, there was a steeliness in his eyes that hadn't been there before. All shock had disappeared. "She must have thought you ready to leave."

Only a fool would have missed his evasiveness, but I suspected he would not divulge anything to me. I let it slide. The answer to that question wasn't as important as others, and I wanted to save my battles for those.

"Who were my parents?" I asked.

He glanced at Langley. "He didn't tell you?"

So Langley *did* know. I gave him a sharp glare that he accepted with an apologetic nod but no explanation. Sometimes I got the feeling I was an ingredient in a grand experiment that Langley was conducting.

"A poor woman brought you to Langley and Tate's laboratory. She said her husband had worked in the factory next door, but died just before your birth. She was destitute and asked them to keep you until she could afford to feed you."

"Why them? Why not a foundling hospital or church?"

"She said her husband had noticed them often on his way to the factory and had told her how kind and generous they seemed. Apparently one of them had helped an elderly gentleman when he fell in the street, and another time, they'd donated money to the widow of a man who'd been run over by a coach outside their house. She thought they'd be as good to her baby as any organization. You must understand, those institutions don't have very good reputations."

"So I've heard." Yet it still seemed an extraordinary thing for a mother to do. I doubt I could give up a baby to complete strangers, and men too. Then again, I wasn't a mother. "What happened to her?"

"She died soon afterwards."

I pressed a hand to my chest where a piercing pain was trying to burrow through it. I'd thought my parents were long dead, but a small hope had remained in the corner of my heart. Having that hope extinguished once and for all felt like a small part of me had been gouged out with a sharp knife. It hurt.

Jack moved closer. My skin warmed, and I was grateful for the sad smile of sympathy he offered. Lord Wade seemed to notice him for the first time too. His gaze flicked between Jack and Langley, but when Langley offered no introduction, he looked to me again.

"It soon became clear that Tate couldn't be trusted around you," Wade went on. "He wanted to test his experiments on you. As if you were an animal," he spat. "It was horrifying."

"Is that how...I became this way?"

"Yes. He injected you with a substance, and you became a fire maker. He had already injected himself."

"But why?"

He looked to Langley.

"He wanted to be powerful," Langley said. "He isolated a compound that allowed humans to set fire to things at will. He wanted that power for himself, so he injected it into his body. Unfortunately it proved to be unreliable, but when he tried to remove the compound, he couldn't. He needed to create an antidote instead, but that required human experiments and he'd become averse to testing things on himself."

"A little late for that," Wade muttered.

"When you came along, Hannah, Reuben saw a way out of his problem. He injected the compound into you and would have tested his antidote on you too, but I discovered what he was doing by then and took you away."

"Bloody hell," Jack muttered. "He's mad."

My spine tingled. The hairs on the back of my neck rose. I was an experiment gone wrong. Oh. My. God.

"Appalling," Wade said. "When Langley brought you to me and explained what you were capable of, I was shocked, but I was determined to keep you safe from Tate."

"How noble of you." It came out harsh, but I was still reeling from all I'd learned. Not only was I most certainly an orphan, I was used as a test case by a madman. It was almost too much to fathom.

"You must understand something," Wade said. "My mistress's baby…" He swallowed. "It died some years earlier. I was still coming to terms with that when you came along. I couldn't allow another baby to suffer."

"Then why, three years later, was I relegated to the attic with Vi?"

"It was Lady Wade's wish."

"Is it because Eugenia was born?"

"In part. You were quite a handful, you see. You had a terrible temper at that age, and every time you threw a tantrum, the sparks set something alight. It was becoming harder and harder to hide the fact from the servants. Lady Wade found it exhausting. It wrecked her nerves. I tried to tell her that it wasn't your fault, that you were unique and needed special care, but she wouldn't listen."

Jack opened his mouth to say something, perhaps comment that I wasn't so unique, but closed it again when his uncle held up his hand for silence. Wade didn't see it. He was too busy looking down at his lap.

"If it was me your wife didn't like, why did you confine Vi to the attic too? There's nothing wrong with her. You let me believe she was the one starting the fires, yet it was me all along. So why lock her away too? Your own *daughter*?"

"I'll not speak of Violet," he said, lifting his chin and pursing his lips beneath the shrubbery of his moustache. "If she has questions, she can ask me herself."

I'd hoped to gain some insight as to whether Vi was indeed his daughter at all, but he gave none, and I doubted he would tell me outright. It was certainly strange that he would lock away his legitimate and perfectly normal child.

"Will you at least tell me if she's still in the attic?"

The moustache moved as he thought through his answer. "She's as free as any girl her age."

My throat closed as my heart swelled. I'd thought myself immune to gentle feelings where Vi was concerned, but it seemed I was not. To think she was free! I was so happy for her.

I wondered how she liked it. Vi was always such a nervous girl that part of me thought she may have wanted to remain in the attic. But that was absurd. No one would want that.

"I'm glad to hear it, my lord," I said. "Did you let her out because I'd left?"

He hesitated again before answering. "I thought it was time. Now, is there anything else, or may I leave?"

"I haven't finished."

"I'm a very busy man, Hannah." The disdain and impatience had returned to his tone. The earl had taken over from the man again. I was sorry to see it, and not only because it meant it would be harder to get answers from him now, but also because I liked the man and not the earl better.

"Who put the hypnosis block on me?"

It was terribly satisfying to see the color drain from his face. He looked quite ashen and much older. "Ah. Yes." He looked to Langley who merely waited for an answer too. "That was on the advice of a gentleman from the Society. He thought it best if you didn't know what you were capable of. A way of keeping you sane, if you like. He put the block in place himself."

"He's a hypnotist? What was his name?"

"Myer."

"Was he a natural hypnotist?" It was a question asked for Samuel's benefit, but Wade merely shrugged.

"I don't know what you're talking about," he said. "He hypnotized you so that you would fall asleep whenever you emitted fire. When you woke up, you remembered nothing. I don't regret having him do it, if that's what you wish to know. The fire used to frighten you, and you'd scream until you were hoarse. After the hypnosis, you became a placid little thing most of the time. Much easier to manage."

It seemed a rather callous thing to do to a child. Then again, so was confining her to an attic.

"I do believe she's run out of questions," Langley said. "Are you sure you won't stay for tea, Wade?"

"I don't think you really want me to," Wade said with a sneer.

Langley smiled in that twisted way he had. "No, but it's the polite thing to ask. I do my best to fit into society's requirements for the owner of Frakingham."

Wade stood and squared his shoulders, making himself even taller, especially when Langley had to remain in his wheelchair. "You'll never be anything more than a scientist."

Langley laughed, but even I could tell it was hollow. Langley was a proud, intelligent man with grand aspirations. He would not like to be put in his place by anyone, let alone someone he must consider intellectually inferior.

Lord Wade strode out of the room. I followed him to the door where Tommy waited to see him out. "Will you tell Violet you saw me?" I asked.

He accepted his coat and gloves from Tommy. "I'll tell her you're safe. She'll want to know that much."

"Can she come here to see me? Or I her?"

He pointed his gloves at me and shook them. "Do not come anywhere near Windamere Manor, Hannah. I don't want you seeing Violet. Do you hear me? She has a new life and so do you. I can see that you belong here among these people. It would serve neither of you any good to meet now.

49

Understand?"

Tears pricked my eyes, but I held them back. I walked to the door and opened it myself. The cool breeze was sheer relief on my hot skin and helped calm me a little. "Speaking of not being welcome," I said.

His moustache twitched with indignation.

Tommy offered him his hat, as Lord Wade reached for it, he pulled it back. He strode to the door and threw it down the steps.

"Good day, milord." Tommy bowed as Lord Wade stormed past him. He slammed the door shut and winked at me. "You look like you could do with a cup of tea."

CHAPTER 4

Our efforts in the attic produced nothing but dust and cobwebs. We abandoned the search at lunchtime after which Jack and I retreated to our training room. It was a small room situated at the top of the southern wing. The walls were covered with woolen hangings, the floor with woolen rugs, and most of the furniture had been removed. It was sparse, grim, and well suited to be occupied by someone who couldn't control her fiery temper.

I hated it. It was horribly similar to the attic I'd lived in at Windamere Manor. The difference was, those rooms were my entire life. Aside from the brief walks we could take on occasion, Vi and I had not been allowed out of the stark parlor and bedroom. At least at Frakingham, I was only holed up for an afternoon here and there. Our training sessions had grown shorter each day. We seemed to be making no progress at all, something that frustrated not only Jack and myself, but August Langley too. I wasn't sure if that was because he wanted me to be in control of my fire, or because he wanted me to leave. Our agreement had been that I was free to go once I'd learned to control my affliction like Jack.

"You still seem a little rattled," Jack said when we were alone together.

"Seeing Lord Wade again was more disturbing than I'd expected it to be. I've never spoken to him like that before. Never dared confront him or question him." I tried hard to sort through my feelings where Wade was concerned. On the one hand, he was the austere head of a grand household, but on the other, he was the only father figure I'd ever had. He may have been a largely absent one, but he didn't need to be in the same room as me to have an influence over my life.

"He wasn't as intimidating as I thought he'd be," I said.

"Perhaps because you're harder to intimidate now."

"What do you mean?"

He sat on a footstool across from me and rested his elbows on his knees. His eyes turned soft and a smile hovered on his lips but didn't break free. "You're not a child anymore. You've seen and done things in the few short weeks of your freedom that most women haven't seen and done in a lifetime. You've changed, Hannah, and your perception of things and people has changed too."

"I suppose so." It wasn't only because of the new experiences I had every day, but also because of my fire. I wasn't a weakling who fell asleep at the slightest provocation as I used to think, but a fire starter. It gave me a kind of power, even if I couldn't control it. "I won't let men like Lord Wade intimidate me again."

"I know." He traced his fingertip down my knee and a spark shot onto my dress. He extinguished it before it did anything more than scorch the fabric, but I still felt the responding heat rise within me.

"Sorry," he said, bitterness threading the word. "I couldn't help myself." He rose and paced the room, dragging his hands through his hair. "I hate this, Hannah. I'm going to go crazy if I can't…you know."

It felt like claws raked my heart, leaving an exposed, throbbing wound. I wanted him to caress me and hold me, and I wanted to hold him in return, but there was nothing that could be done. Perhaps one day when I learned to control the fire, I could also control it during tender moments with him, but that day seemed a long way off.

I stood up in front of him, halting his pacing. "Jack—"

"Don't!"

He turned to the window and stared out at the lake and abbey ruins on the other side of the park. It was early afternoon. The muted light made the scenery look like a painting. We stood side by side yet far enough apart to avoid sparks and stared out at the winter quiet together. After a few moments I felt my face cool, my blood calm. I'd not realized how hot I was.

"We'll find a way," I eventually said. "No matter how long it takes."

He sighed. "Until then, I must go swimming. Lots and lots of swimming."

"It cools you down?"

"Oh yes."

Like almost everything he tried, Jack was an excellent swimmer. I liked to stand on the lake's edge and watch him glide through the water. It soothed me as much as it seemed to soothe him. He'd once asked me to join him, but I'd refused. I couldn't swim and had no intention of getting into a deep body of water. The hideous bathing costume Sylvia had shown me in one of her copies of *The Young Ladies' Journal* made the decision easier.

Besides, there would be no wandering near the lake or anywhere else while that demon was on the loose. Langley had given strict instructions that everyone was to remain inside. The gardeners had been given time off. Even Olsen took Jack with him when he tended the horses.

"I wonder where it is," I said.

"I wish I knew."

A piercing, unnatural scream answered us.

"Bloody hell!" Jack sprinted out the door and raced down the stairs.

I followed, but couldn't keep up. "Don't go outside!" I

called after him.

He didn't answer. I heard the door unlock and crash back on its hinges. When I finally reached it, he was long gone. He was so fast that I didn't have a hope of catching him.

Sylvia rushed up to me and slipped her arm around my waist. "Has he gone after it?"

I nodded.

"Such a pig-headed fool! Why can't he let the authorities do it? It's their job after all."

"They'll have even less chance of catching it than he does." I believed what I said, yet I didn't like Jack being out there any more than she did.

Tommy joined us. He carried a piece of firewood as long and thick as his forearm and the smell of animal grease followed him. In his other hand, he carried a box of matches to light the grease that must be smeared on the end of the wood.

"Which direction did he take?" he asked.

"You're not going after him!" Sylvia declared. "It's much too dangerous."

"I can't let Jack do this alone."

Sylvia stood between him and the door.

"Move aside, Miss Langley."

She put her hand on her hip. "You will have to move me yourself."

He set the wood and matches down and, to Sylvia's horror, picked her up.

"Stop! Put me down!" She pounded her fists against his shoulder, but her blows had no effect whatsoever. "Tommy Dawson, I'm ordering you to put me down this instant!"

"As you wish, Miss Langley." He carried her to the staircase and set her on the bottom step. I rather think he enjoyed disobeying. He certainly looked too cheerful for someone about to venture outside with a dangerous creature on the loose.

"Uncle will hear how you manhandled me."

"I doubt it," he muttered under his breath as he passed

me.

"I don't think it's wise to go out," I said as he picked up his torch and matches.

"Do you want Jack to do this on his own, Miss Smith?"

I couldn't meet his steady gaze. Of course I didn't, but I didn't want to send anyone else out there either.

Tommy left before Sylvia could reach him and drag him back inside. She stamped her foot on the floor and glared at the door as if she'd rip it off its hinges.

"I'll have to tell Uncle. He cannot be allowed to speak to me like that, Hannah, and he certainly shouldn't be touching me." She pressed a hand to her heart and stretched her neck, tilting her chin out. "It's wrong. He's a footman, and I am the niece of his employer. He should remember his place."

Samuel came through the arched entrance to one of the corridors. "So you two heard it?"

"Yes," I said. "Jack and Tommy have gone after it."

"Tommy too?" He shook his head. "Bloody fool."

"He took a torch," Sylvia said with a sniff. "He's no fool."

First she railed at him for following Jack, and then she defended him. I understood her about as well as I understood her uncle.

"He'll be all right," she added and walked off, hugging herself. "They both will."

I stood by the window, but the view was limited on the ground floor. Upstairs would be better and I told Samuel so.

"Why not come into the parlor where it's warmer?" he said.

"I don't need warmth."

"Oh. Of course. Right. The fire thing." He shook his head and followed me up the stairs. "I'm still puzzled by your…ability. It's so extraordinary that I can't quite fathom it. My poor scientific brain has trouble comprehending things that can't be explained."

"Your hypnosis ability can't be explained," I pointed out.

"Beside that."

"August Langley seems to have no such trouble, and he's

a scientist."

"That puzzles me even more. The man is a curiosity. For example, how did his involvement in the supernatural come about?"

"I don't know. Why not ask him?"

He snorted. "I have. He refused to answer. I also asked him why he took both you and Jack in. Again, I received no answer. Do you know, Hannah?"

"Jack is his nephew!" Although I had my suspicions on that score, I wasn't ready to confide in Samuel. It wasn't his business. It wasn't even mine.

"What about you?" he asked. "Why are you living here?"

"I told you what Lord Wade said to me yesterday. I suppose Langley feels some responsibility toward me since he was the one who placed me in Wade's care. When he learned I was in the attic, he must have felt compelled to retrieve me." Except he hadn't known I was in the attic. Not then. Later, yes. Clearly I hadn't been abducted for any charitable reasons, despite what he said. "He thought it time to teach me to control the fire."

"And how is that going?"

I reached the landing on the top-most floor and turned to face him. "As well as can be expected."

He stood one step down from me, yet he was still taller, and cocked his head to the side. "That is not an answer."

"Speaking of taking people in, why has Langley allowed *you* to live here, Samuel?"

"He's a patron of the sciences and sees my research as having merit."

"You've not yet explained what your research is about except to say it involves the human mind."

"I wouldn't want to confuse you."

It was my turn to cock my head to the side. "You think a woman can't comprehend it? I'd not thought you so prejudiced against the female sex."

His eyebrows lifted. "It has nothing to do with you being female and everything to do with you not being a scientist."

"*Humph.*" I spun round and stalked off toward the training room.

He followed. "Come now, Hannah, let's not quarrel." His tone was soothing, melodic. Hypnotic. "We've been such good friends ever since we met. I'd like to keep it that way."

"Don't try to hypnotize me, Samuel Gladstone."

He reached around me and opened the door. "Don't, Hannah," he said heavily. "I would never do such a thing without your consent. Not anymore."

I swallowed, nodded. "I'm sorry. I know you wouldn't employ unscrupulous methods."

"I hope you mean that. If you don't believe me, there's no hope that anyone else in this house will."

Where before he sounded fully in command of himself, now he sounded somewhat morose. I took his hand and squeezed a smile out of him, albeit a sad one.

We watched for some time out of the training room window. Sylvia joined us, carrying a tray of tea and cakes that she and Samuel ate. I didn't feel hungry, which troubled Sylvia.

"You're too thin, and lately you seem quite gaunt around the cheeks. You should eat. Tell her, Samuel."

"She's right, Hannah, but I'm sure you have a lot on your mind right now."

Sylvia huffed at him. "That was hardly a convincing argument. Perhaps you could try hypnotizing her and ordering her to eat something."

He winced. "That is quite unethical."

"Not to mention unhealthy," I added. "What if I overeat?"

"Then you'll have a nice plump figure," Sylvia said. "You could do with some fattening in…certain areas."

I gave her a withering glare while Samuel looked out the window, no doubt pretending not to know that she was referring to my chest.

"Here they come!" he shouted, leaping off his chair.

We peered past him. Jack and Tommy approached the

house together, their arms around each other's shoulders. It wasn't until they drew closer that I realized Tommy was limping and Jack was helping him.

Sylvia gave a little squeal and raced out of the room. Samuel and I followed her down the stairs to the door as Jack and Tommy entered. Blood darkened a gash in Tommy's trouser leg, and he winced as he set pressure on his left foot.

"You stupid, foolish, idiotic *idiot*!" Sylvia shouted. "You deserve that for going outside when I warned you not to." Her fists pumped at her sides, and her face turned red. If she had my affliction, she'd have set the entrance hall on fire by now. "Take him into the parlor and put his leg up. Fetch some water, cloths and bandages." When she realized there were no servants present except the injured Tommy, she clicked her tongue and sent Samuel off to find the supplies.

Jack helped Tommy into the parlor and sat him down. I pushed a footstool closer and he rested his injured leg upon it. "What happened?"

"I was searching through the woods," Jack said, "looking for signs of the demon being near. I found the deer that must have been its last meal."

"Oh, the poor thing."

"I was following what I think were its tracks when I heard Tommy calling my name. When I reached him, I saw the demon crouch, preparing to attack. It pounced before my fireball reached it."

"But you stopped it from doing anything worse." Tommy rolled up his torn trouser leg, revealing four bloody gashes below the knee. The scratches were even in length and width apart, and could only have been made by a claw.

Sylvia plopped down on the settee, her face white. All her anger and indignation had drained away, leaving an empty shell.

"I was just poking around the woods," Tommy said. "I found nothing and was about to come back when it came out of nowhere."

"That's because it's invisible," Sylvia said, showing signs of life again. "You already knew that, and yet you still went."

"It's not invisible anymore," Jack said.

"What?"

I sat down beside Sylvia. Both of us stared at him. "What do you mean?" I asked.

"I saw it," Tommy said. "Not until it was too late, but I still saw it."

"Was it as Jack described?"

He and Jack exchanged glances. "Not exactly. It looked...a little more human."

Sylvia caught my hand. I gave hers a reassuring squeeze, but I felt no reassurance myself. "Would you care to elaborate?" I said.

Tommy shook his head.

Sylvia sniffed and I held her hand tighter.

Samuel came in with Langley, wheeled by Bollard. "Mrs. Moore wanted to tend the wound," Samuel said, "but I told her it wasn't too bad and that one of you ladies would do it. I didn't think we wanted her to overhear our conversation." He held out the supplies to Sylvia and me.

She didn't seem in any fit state to tend anything so I took the bowl of water and dampened the cloth. I didn't know what I was doing, but I did know the wound needed to be cleaned if only to see how bad it was. Tommy winced and sucked air through his teeth, but I managed to remove the blood.

"I don't think it's too deep," I said, inspecting the gashes.

"From now on, no one goes anywhere without Jack," Langley said, speaking for the first time. "If anybody leaves this house again without my permission, their pay will be docked. Understand?" His glare and his words were aimed rather sharply at Tommy.

The footman lowered his head and nodded. To my surprise, Sylvia didn't seem at all triumphant that she'd got her wish. Relieved, yes, but not happy.

I wound a length of bandage around the wound, eliciting

more wincing from Tommy.

"If it's not caught by the time you all must leave for the trial, then those of us remaining behind will have to manage without Jack," Langley said. "We can stock up on supplies before you leave and dismiss the servants. With only Samuel and me here anyway, they won't be needed."

"I'd forgotten about the trial," Sylvia muttered.

Reuben Tate was scheduled for trial the following week. Jack, Sylvia, Tommy and I were to be called as witnesses. The detective inspector in charge of the case said it wasn't likely to take long and would result in a verdict of guilty. He was absolutely certain. It was such a relief to have it almost over. Perhaps that was why I'd felt so on edge lately and somewhat exhausted. Just thinking about our ordeal with Tate was both tiring and terrifying.

"Samuel, help Tommy to his room," Langley said. "Sylvia, fetch me my smoking jacket and slippers, please. I'm cold."

The three of them left, leaving just Jack, Langley, Bollard and me. I suspected there was a reason the others had been sent away, and I didn't have to wait long to find out what it was.

"How is your training coming along?" Langley asked. "Any progress?"

"None," Jack said.

"Hannah, do you feel like something has shifted within you?"

"What do you mean?"

"Do you feel different in any way, even small?"

I shook my head. "I feel exactly the same. I am happier, I suppose."

"Happier?"

"Being here with Jack, Sylvia and Samuel is much better than being locked away at Windamere. I do miss Vi sometimes, and I do feel more tired from all the training and the worry about the trial and now the demon, but overall I'm happy. Knowing what I am is an enormous relief, as is no longer being a narcolpetic."

He grunted. "I don't want you to be happy. I want you cured."

"Thank you, I think. It's kind of you to worry about me."

"Don't read sentimentality into it. I want you cured because I want you gone. You're disruptive. I had no idea it would be like this."

His words were like a slap across the face. They stung. I could do nothing but stare at him, my mouth open. I was entirely lost for words.

"Speak to her like that again, August, and you'll get your wish," Jack said. He spoke levelly, quietly, but the hard edge was unmistakable. "She'll leave, but I'll go with her. Neither of us is bound to stay here."

Was it my imagination, or did Langley's face pale? His tongue darted out and licked his lower lip. "You can't leave. You're dependent upon my good will. What would you do for money? Return to being a thief and a liar?"

"I'd find work. I have an education now and experience running this estate. I've been thinking about finding employment anyway. Hannah could come with me and Sylvia too. You can stay here with Bollard. I'm sure the two of you would be very happy on your own."

Langley's nostrils flared. He pressed his hands to the arms of his wheelchair as if he would lift himself out of it and confront Jack face to face. "Bollard, take me out."

Bollard did as ordered. Where his master's face looked ravaged with anger and frustration, Bollard's was its usual blank mask. I wondered if they ever discussed things of a personal nature in the privacy of Langley's room. Although Bollard couldn't speak, he could communicate with his hands. But I doubted they did. Neither seemed like the sort to connect on a personal level.

"Wait," Langley said.

Langley put his hand up at the door and Bollard stopped and turned the wheelchair to face us. "Don't forget you agreed to remain here until Christmas, Hannah."

"I haven't forgotten." I wasn't sure whether he was reminding me because he couldn't wait for Christmas to arrive and be rid of me, or because he didn't want me to leave *before* I was cured.

Bollard wheeled him out, and I let out a long, measured breath. Dealing with Langley was always an ordeal, but I felt more drained than usual.

"Are you all right?" Jack asked, frowning at me.

I nodded. "He took me by surprise. I didn't think he was so against me being here."

"Nor did I. I actually thought he liked having you around for Sylvia's sake. I wonder what has changed his mind."

"I doubt we'll ever know."

"Perhaps I should talk to him about it."

I snorted softly. "I wish you luck with that endeavor. You're going to need it."

He sat on the settee beside me, his long legs stretched out. "Whatever his reason for wanting you gone, he has no right to speak to you in such a manner. I won't stand for it."

"Don't take it personally. Langley seems to speak to everyone as if they're beneath him. Sometimes I think he puts Bollard above us all."

That brought a smile to his lips. "That's what I like about you. You're so forgiving, even of someone like August."

"Why do you call him August and not Uncle like Sylvia? I know I've asked you before, but you never gave me a satisfactory answer."

He shrugged. "I was fourteen when I came here. That's a lot of years in which I thought I had no family. It took a long time to become used to being part of a real one. I suppose I just can't think of him as my uncle. I'm still not certain he even is my relation at all anyway."

"You may have thought you had no family, but you had Tommy and the other boys. He's as devoted to you as any brother. That's family, Jack. Perhaps even a truer one than whatever it is August Langley has created here."

He stretched his arm across the back of the settee behind

me. "You may be right. I'm finding that you often are."

I felt the familiar rush of warmth through my body, the sort that wasn't brought on by the fire within but by Jack's gentle words and intense gazes. It was happening quite often lately.

"Are *you* all right?" I asked him. "The demon didn't hurt you, did it?"

"I'm fine, but I don't mind telling you that I'm worried. How are we going to get rid of a demon? I feel utterly useless. It's not a state I'm familiar with."

"Langley sent a letter back with the policemen to post to Mr. and Mrs. Beaufort. With any luck they'll respond quickly. Until then, we must avoid it and warn the villagers to stay away from here. Not that they make frequent visits, but still."

"You're right again," he said. "There are deer and other animals in the woods to satisfy its hunger for a while. Hopefully it won't venture closer to the village or the house."

I certainly hoped he was right.

***

With the house tightly locked up and no one allowed to leave, it came as an enormous surprise when someone knocked on the door early the next morning. Maud the housemaid opened it since Tommy was incapacitated. She brought the visitor into the parlor where Jack, Samuel, Sylvia and I sat talking.

"Detective Inspector Weeks from the Harborough Constabulary to see you, Mr. Langley," she announced then retreated.

The thin, sharp-cheeked inspector held his hat in his hands and looked decidedly uncomfortable in our presence. Or perhaps he was uncomfortable being inside Freak House. He did glance about rather nervously as if he expected ghouls to emerge from the very walls.

"Is this about the wild dog, Inspector?" Jack prompted. "I told you everything I knew."

"Has it hurt someone else?" Sylvia asked, lowering her embroidery hoop to her lap.

"No, ma'am, and I'm not here about the wild dog, sir. I called off the search in actual fact. My men found no sign of it the day of the attack, so I reckon it must have left the area. Besides, I don't have the men available to poke around the woods no more."

He was a fool to think it was gone, but none of us gainsaid him. His men were much safer away from the woods altogether. We'd just been discussing how to broach the subject with the police before the inspector arrived. It was most fortunate that he was ahead of us for once. He wasn't known for his thoroughness, something Jack had discovered the long and hard way a few weeks earlier when he'd tried to get Weeks to accompany him to London to confront Tate. Weeks had refused.

"Then how may we help you?" Jack asked.

Weeks patted his coat pockets. When he didn't find what he was looking for, he set his hat down on a table and used both hands. "It's here somewhere," he said. "I know it is."

"What is?" Sylvia asked.

"The telegram."

"You have a telegram for me?" Jack said.

"No, sir."

When he continued to pat and not elaborate, Jack persisted. "For August Langley then?"

At the mention of the name, Weeks paused in his search and glanced nervously at the door. "Is he here, your uncle?"

"He's working. So the telegram *is* for him?"

"Hmmm, what?" The inspector returned his attention to an inside pocket of his coat. "No, it's not for Mr. August Langley. It's just that I haven't seen him since he moved in except for that one time when his papers were stolen some weeks ago. The lads at the station will want to know if I spoke to him again. Not to mention Mrs. Weeks. She likes to know what goes on in the village and up here at the big house. Lucky she married the local inspector, eh?"

"My uncle is not a sideshow act, Inspector Weeks," Sylvia snapped. "Now if you don't mind, either hand over the telegram, or tell us its contents. That's if you can remember what it said."

Her scolding was quite lost on the policeman as he continued to burrow deep into his pockets a second time.

"It can't be for me," Samuel said. "Nobody even knows I'm here."

That was news to me. I was about to ask him why he'd never informed his family, but Inspector Weeks pulled a piece of paper out of his pocket and waved it triumphantly.

"Here it is! It was addressed to me at the station and asks me to come to Frakingham immediately and give you the news."

"What news?" Sylvia asked at the same time that Jack said, "Who is it from?"

Weeks held the paper close to his face and squinted hard. "It's from Scotland Yard."

Jack held out his hand for the telegram, and Weeks handed it over. Jack read it and promptly sat down.

"What does it say?" I asked, leaning forward.

Sylvia shifted to face him and the hoop slid off her lap to the floor. "Jack, you're scaring us," she said.

He cleared his throat. "It says Reuben Tate has escaped from Newgate Prison."

CHAPTER 5

I felt everyone's gaze upon me. They didn't need to voice their anxiety and concern because it was there in their eyes and the deep grooves of worry across their foreheads. It echoed within me. Tate had escaped...and he would come after me, the one person he thought could help him find a cure for his fire starting.

It was only a matter of time.

Inspector Weeks did not look my way like the others. He was busy talking and folding the paper on which the telegram was written. "I'm sure they'll catch him soon," he said. "They're very good at Scotland Yard. Very good. Matter of fact, they've probably already got him and locked him up again. No need to worry yourselves just yet, but it's better to be forewarned, I always say."

"Yes," I said, my voice sounding distant and small. I stared down at my hands in my lap because I could no longer stand seeing everyone's faces. My knuckles were white. I unclenched my fists and flattened my palms over my skirt. My hands shook.

"Thank you, Inspector," Samuel said. He seemed the only one of us capable of saying anything useful. Sylvia appeared to be having difficulty breathing, and Jack was lost in thought. He stared at the floor as if he could find Tate's whereabouts written there.

"I'll send word if there's any more news," Weeks said. He put the telegram back in his pocket and reached for his hat. "Good day, ladies, gentlemen."

"I'll see you out," Samuel said.

"Wait!" Jack moved to stand between Weeks and the door.

Weeks, caught by surprise, stepped back, almost bumping into Samuel. "Yes, Mr. Langley?"

"Hannah's life may be in danger from Tate. You need to send men to protect her."

"I'm sure he won't come here, Mr. Langley. If he hasn't been caught already, then he'll most likely be making his away to the nearest port and a ship to America. That's what I'd do if I were him."

"You're not him," Jack ground out through a rigid jaw. "And I'm telling you that he *will* come looking for Hannah. She needs protecting."

"Now listen here, Mr. Langley. I don't have men to spare to laze about up here dining on fancy dinners and sipping tea all afternoon. We're very busy in Harborough. If there was an immediate threat to Miss Smith's safety, then I wouldn't hesitate. Like I said, Mr. Tate is probably already out of the country."

"Thank you, Inspector," I said quickly, eyeing Jack's fingers. He looked like he was about to set off sparks in Weeks's direction. "You're right, there's no need to worry yet."

Weeks frowned. "Why are you only concerned for Miss Smith's safety?" he asked Jack, oblivious to the fire he was stoking. "You were all going to give evidence, weren't you? I'd have thought he'd come for all of you, not just her." We'd apprised Weeks of the situation upon our return from London after Tate's arrest. It seemed he'd listened after all.

Sylvia gave a little cry of distress. Samuel cleared his

throat. "If he wasn't on his way to America by now you mean," he said.

"Right you are, sir." Weeks slapped his hat on his head. "It's Mr. Gladstone, isn't it? I heard there was another gentleman residing up here." He gave Samuel a thorough once-over as if he were trying to fathom why someone would voluntarily live at Freak House.

Samuel raised his eyebrows. "Good day, Inspector."

Jack stepped aside and Weeks cleared his throat. "Right. Yes. Good day to you all."

Samuel walked him out, and Jack watched him go. After a moment, he strode up to the fireplace and shot a small fireball into the grate. The flames leapt and danced wildly before settling down again.

"Feel better?" I said, trying to sound light.

"I can't believe this," he growled. "Incompetent fools."

"Don't be too harsh. I'm sure Tate used his fire to get himself out."

"I wouldn't be so certain. Could you have become angry enough to start a fire if you were in a filthy prison cell, waiting for your life to end?"

Like me, Tate needed to be angry to summon the fire. We couldn't produce sparks at will like Jack. "I suppose you're right," I said, "but I'm not Reuben Tate. It's possible he found something to fuel his temper. He struck me as a rather volatile man."

"That is quite the understatement," Sylvia muttered.

Jack shook his head and headed for the door. "I'm not so sure."

"Where are you going?"

"Into the village to send a telegram to Scotland Yard. I want to know more about how he escaped and what they're doing to find him. Besides, it's too dangerous for Weeks to travel alone back to Harborough. The man's a fool, but I don't want his blood on my hands. I also want to press home the need for the villagers to be careful until further notice."

I'd not thought it possible, but I'd forgotten about the

demon. "You be careful too, Jack."

"I will. I'll take my knife just in case. I don't know if it'll stop it entirely, but I don't want to use the fire unless absolutely necessary."

He left just as Bollard wheeled Langley in, not giving Sylvia or me a moment to discuss what had happened.

"I saw that inspector arrive," Langley said.

Sylvia ran to her uncle and gave him an awkward embrace. "Oh, Uncle, it's awful! Tate has escaped."

Langley's face froze. His nostrils flared. Even Bollard's eyes widened and turned on me. His expression—any expression—was so unexpected that I shrank back into the cushioned seat of the settee.

"It's terrible," Sylvia said, holding onto her uncle's hand. Langley seemed to not want to let her go, which wasn't at all like him. Signs of affection between himself and his niece and nephew were rare.

"Where is Jack going? Bollard, fetch him. He needs to stay here to protect Hannah."

Yesterday he'd wanted me to leave the house as soon as I was in control of my fire. Today he seemed distressed that any harm would come to me. Trying to understand him was impossible.

Of course, his sudden change may have nothing to do with wanting me to be safe and everything to do with not wanting Reuben Tate to get hold of the one thing that could lead him to a cure—me. There was a history between them, and I had no doubt they were rivals in their work. It was possible that I'd become a pawn in that rivalry.

"Wait, Bollard," I said. To my surprise, the mute obeyed and stopped. "Jack has gone to find out more, and I think we should let him go. Without details, we could make a wrong step. He won't be long."

Langley closed his eyes. I thought he was controlling his temper or perhaps trying to block me out, but after a moment he nodded. "Very well. Where's Samuel and Tommy?"

"Tommy is injured, Uncle," Sylvia said. "Remember?"

"He has a few scratches, that's all. What about Samuel? It's up to him to check that all the doors and windows are locked."

"They already are," I said. "Because of the demon." Had he forgotten about it already? He did seem quite flustered.

Langley glared at me. "Take me out, Bollard."

Bollard wheeled his master out of the parlor, leaving Sylvia and me to stare after them.

"I don't think I'll ever understand your uncle," I said.

She sighed and came to sit by me again. "It's not his fault. His mind works differently to everyone else's."

It certainly did. What wasn't so certain was whether that difference was a good thing or bad.

***

Our nerves remained frayed until Jack finally walked in after night fell. He went to see Langley then met us in the dining room. We'd already started our soup course, but it was still warm in the tureen. Maud filled a bowl for him.

"Well?" Sylvia prompted as soon as he sat. "Did you receive a response from Scotland Yard?"

"Tate hasn't been found," Jack said.

Sylvia dropped her spoon and pressed her napkin to her mouth. Samuel swore quietly. My gaze connected with Jack's, and I nodded for him to go on.

"Tate's man Ham escaped too," he said.

"Really?" Samuel said. "Extraordinary."

"How did it happen?" I asked, not wanting to mention fire in front of Maud. Tommy was the only servant aware of our supernatural abilities and all the circumstances surrounding our conflict with Tate.

"Ham escaped from his cell by killing one of the guards. He then freed Tate."

"But…how?" Samuel frowned. "There would have been several more guards, plus locks and heavy doors to pass through. Newgate is a warren of cells and corridors."

"How do you know?" Sylvia asked.

Samuel's only answer to that was a shrug. "Even if he managed to get both himself and Tate free, he would have had to scale the external walls. They're incredibly high."

"It does seem rather extraordinary," I said.

"Yet it *has* happened." Sylvia pushed her soup away. "The method is unimportant, but the fact remains, they have escaped and are out there somewhere."

"That's enough, Sylvia," Jack said with a glance at Maud. "You'll frighten everyone."

"I think Reuben Tate is doing a rather good job of that too." She pulled her bowl back and tasted her soup.

I exchanged a worried glance with Jack. "I'm moving into the room next to yours," he said to me.

Sylvia's spoon hit the side of her bowl with a clank. "I don't think that's necessary. Nor is it appropriate. I doubt Uncle will be pleased."

"Maud, will you tell Mrs. Moore to make up the spare bedroom." Jack waited until the maid had left before going on. "Syl, you can move into my room. No one should be near Hannah except me."

"I can help," Samuel said. "I used to fight at university."

"Boxing?"

"More or less."

What the devil did that mean?

"I can protect her," Jack said.

Samuel shrugged. "If you change your mind, let me know."

We discussed the arrangements until Maud returned. She collected our bowls and served the main meal. Usually only footmen served, but these were extraordinary circumstances and Frakingham an extraordinary household. She did a good job of it too. Her only mistake was to serve from the wrong side. Of course Sylvia picked up on the error immediately and corrected her.

When dinner was over and we'd adjourned to the parlor, she brought the mistake up again. "When will Tommy return to his regular duties? Uncle was right when he said he only

71

has a few scratches. You said yourself they weren't deep, Hannah. Couldn't he return to light duties tomorrow?"

"Miss him, do you?" Samuel teased, sitting down with a glass of whiskey.

"Of course I do. I miss him standing on my *left*. Maud is a good girl and is trying hard, but it's not the same."

"She's not a girl," I said. "She's older than us."

"All housemaids are girls to their employers, Hannah. If they rise to the rank of housekeeper, then we call them women. I know it's not your fault that you don't understand since you didn't have much contact with the servants at Windamere, but there you have it."

I had *no* contact with the servants at Windamere Manor, unless the governess Miss Levine counted. "Thank you for educating me," I said wryly. "The world would come to an end if we let social mores lapse."

She narrowed her gaze. "I know you think that's amusing, but I don't."

"Tommy should rest for a few more days," Jack said, standing by the window.

Sylvia sighed. "I didn't want to say it in front of the poor girl, but Tommy is a much better footman than Maud."

"You do say the stupidest things sometimes, Syl." He turned back to the window and crossed his arms, settling into an evening of surveillance. It was too dark to see much, but he still kept watch for the demon anyway.

The demon *and* Reuben Tate.

***

"But I *need* to deliver them," Sylvia wailed. She and I had spent the evening writing out invitations to our Christmas dinner party, but in the cold light of day, she'd realized she had no way of taking them into the village. She couldn't even ask one of the servants to go since Langley had forbade them to leave while the demon was still on the loose.

"Surely the invitations can wait a few days," Jack said.

"What makes you think any of this will be over in a few days?" she asked, hand on hip. "Honestly, Jack, you are far too optimistic for your own good."

"And you are petulant and irritating. The invitations will have to wait. I'm the only one who can deliver them, and I have to stay here with Hannah."

She clicked her tongue. "Stop being a martyr. If Tommy were up and about he'd not hesitate to do it."

"That's because Tommy can't say no to anything you ask of him. I'm not such a fool."

Jack was about to go out and walk around the house to check that everything was as it should be now that it was morning. After a restless night, I'd gotten out of bed early. Why lie in and worry alone when I could worry in company? I'd come across Sylvia and Jack arguing in the entrance hall.

"Jack's right," I said. "It's too dangerous for anyone to leave the house. The invitations can wait."

"Nonsense," August Langley said as he rolled in, Bollard pushing him. He looked as tired as I felt. Jack and Sylvia also sported dark shadows under their eyes. Clearly no one had slept very well.

"See!" Sylvia cried. "Uncle agrees. The invitations *are* important. If we don't get them out soon, our guests will receive others and accept those instead."

"I don't care about the dinner party," Langley said.

Sylvia's face fell. "Then why?" Her question was echoed by Jack.

"You need some time away from Frakingham."

"Precisely," Sylvia said triumphantly.

"Why?" Jack hedged.

I looked for any sign that Langley was joking, but there was none. The only movement he made was to jerk his head to the side when Bollard cleared his throat, as if he went to glance over his shoulder at his valet but stopped himself.

"Being confined here day in and day out is not good for you young people," Langley said. "You'll be safe if you all go together. Indeed, the village may be the best place for you right now. The demon is in the woods, not near the village, and Tate will come straight here to look for you. Yes." He gave an emphatic nod. "A day in the village it shall be."

Bollard wheeled him away, leaving the three of us staring after him.

"That was very considerate of him," Jack said, clearly skeptical of his uncle's motives if his wary tone was any indication.

"Remarkably so," I said.

"Uncle *can* be a very considerate man," Sylvia said, but didn't sound convinced by her own words. "Do you think he's right and we'll be safe?"

"As long as I'm with Hannah," Jack said. "Besides, we'll be armed."

He left to check the perimeter of the house, and Samuel joined Sylvia and me in the dining room for breakfast. We told him about our trip into the village, and he agreed it was a good idea, but was rather surprised that Langley had come up with it.

"You are all so cynical. Uncle can be very kind." Sylvia paused with bacon halfway to her mouth. "Moderately kind. On the odd occasion."

"I feel sorry for Tommy," Samuel said, buttering his toast. "He would have liked to come. It's not much fun for him in his room all day on his own. Perhaps later he can join us for a game of cribbage."

Sylvia shook her head until she'd swallowed her mouthful of bacon. "Absolutely not. Our circumstances may be unusual at the moment, but rules are rules. A footman simply cannot sit and play cards with us."

"You are such a stickler, Sylvia," Samuel said. "Have a heart. He's terribly bored."

"Perhaps I'll read to him." Her face brightened and her curls bounced with her excitement. "Yes. I will. It's what nurses do for their patients and I am, in essence, his nurse."

"He's quite capable of reading to himself," I said. "His eyes aren't damaged."

She leaned closer to me and whispered, "But *can* he read?"

"He can," I said. "Jack taught him. I'm surprised you weren't aware of that already. After all, I knew and how long have you known him compared to me?" I was teasing, but she didn't take it very well at all. She spluttered an excuse about being too busy to notice footmen. Her face turned a bright shade of red too, all the way to the tips of her ears.

She didn't speak to me again until it was time to head into the village. We met in the entrance hall, and she seemed as bright and cheerful as always. Clearly she'd decided to forgive me. That was one good thing about Sylvia. Her sulks rarely lasted long.

***

We traveled in the coach to Harborough. Samuel sat inside with us, a loaded pistol in his lap. Jack sat on the driver's seat with Olsen, another loaded pistol beside him and his knife tucked in his pocket. Thankfully we didn't need the weapons, and both pistols were stored away in a box beneath our seat when we reached the village.

I always loved our visits to Harborough despite the curious looks we attracted. It was a sizeable village, but pretty with a main central High Street along which almost anything could be found in one of the shops. It followed the course of a stream that babbled its way beneath old stone bridges. Apparently people enjoyed picnics on its banks in summer, but at the moment the banks were more muddy than grassy, and most people kept indoors. I loved the crispness of the air down in the valley and the faint woody scent of smoke frothing out of the chimneys. It was the smell of freedom and seemed to blow away the cobwebs that had taken up residence in my head of late. I felt refreshed, invigorated, and ready to meet new people.

Olsen parked outside the mayor's house, a rather grand-looking building with a gabled roof and bay windows. A child's face appeared at one of the upstairs windows then quickly disappeared again, replaced by the face of a woman wearing a white cap.

Samuel assisted us ladies down the coach steps. Jack soon

joined us. He and I wore coats like the others, and I even pulled on my gloves. The Harborough villagers already thought we were odd. We didn't need to confirm it by not wearing appropriate clothing for wintertime.

"Ready?" Jack asked.

"Ready," Sylvia said. She marched up to the front door and knocked. Samuel, Jack and I stood behind her.

We'd decided to pay informal calls upon our intended guests and deliver our invitations. The Harborough mayor and his wife were the first on our list. Samuel and I were new to them, so Sylvia suggested we introduce ourselves with the hope they'd see how normal we were. She'd also decided that I was a friend of hers who'd come to visit until Christmas. Samuel at least didn't need to lie about his background. He was a neurology student from London taking a sabbatical at Frakingham to conduct research. It was only necessary to avoid the question of how we'd come to know him.

A maid answered the door and showed us through to a parlor that was far too warm for me. A few moments later, Mr. and Mrs. Butterworth entered, identical smiles plastered across their faces. She was a tall woman with a long neck and what could politely be termed strong bone structure. I pegged her to be in her forties, although her dark mourning clothes made her seem older. Mr. Butterworth was shorter than his wife and seemed to have no neck to speak of and soft features. As a couple, they were opposites, or perhaps it would be more polite to say they complemented each other.

Sylvia introduced Samuel and me and handed the invitation to Mrs. Butterworth. She was all bubbling excitement as the mayor's wife opened the thick cream envelope.

"A dinner party!" Mrs. Butterworth said, her eyebrows creeping up her forehead as she read.

"Well," said Mr. Butterworth. "That's—"

"Intriguing," Mrs. Butterworth cut in.

Mr. Butterworth's smile slipped, and he rubbed his hands down his trouser pants. He did not look at his wife.

"Intriguing?" Sylvia prompted.

"What my wife means—"

"What I mean is that there hasn't been a dinner party at Frakingham House in a very long time." Mrs. Butterworth folded the invitation and set it on the table between a framed dried floral picture and a stuffed cat. "A very long time."

Mr. Butterworth coughed and rubbed his hands down his trousers again. If he were annoyed that his wife kept cutting him off, he didn't show it. He continued to smile with what could only be described as fervor. I wondered if that's how he'd won the office of mayor or whether his wife had some influence there. I couldn't imagine him having the constitution required to canvas councilors.

"That's all going to change now that I'm of age," Sylvia said.

"Oh? Have you come out?" Mrs. Butterworth asked.

Sylvia glanced at me in a bit of a panic. "I, uh…"

"Our uncle doesn't go in for ceremony," Jack said, coming to her rescue. "And since Cousin Sylvia has no mother or aunts, there has been no opportunity to organize a coming out occasion."

"Oh." Mrs. Butterworth's thoughts on that could be discerned from the sympathetic gaze. I decided I liked her. She had kind eyes, and although there was curiosity in them too, it did not override more tender feelings. As to her husband, I didn't know what to make of him. He was still smiling in that odd, false way, and he seemed unable to get a full sentence in. I wasn't sure whether to feel sorry for him or irritated that he didn't stand up to her.

"And you, Miss Smith?" Mrs. Butterworth asked. "Have you been presented at court?"

"Alas, my family are not so fortunate to have those lofty connections," I said. "I am out, though. Very, very out."

I could feel Samuel stiffen beside me, and was Jack trying not to smile? Sylvia looked positively horrified, but I was rather pleased with my explanation. I was 'out' of the Windamere Manor attic and that was as 'out' as I would ever be. There would be no balls or afternoon teas for me. I had no family to organize such things. I wasn't even of the right class.

"Where are you from, Miss Smith?" the mayor asked, speaking quickly. No doubt he wanted to get the words out before his wife cut him off.

"Yorkshire," I said, picking a distant county in the hopes they'd not be familiar with it.

"That's—"

"Your accent is remarkably similar to ours," Mrs. Butterworth said.

Oh dear. I had not thought about accents, nor did I know what a Yorkshire one sounded like. That's what I got for lying—a great big mess. "I'm a quick learner," I said. "I've been practicing ever since I arrived."

"Remarkable." I couldn't tell whether she believed me or not, but she didn't ask more questions. She'd already switched her attention to Samuel. "What about you, Mr. Gladstone? You're a doctor?"

"Still studying," he said.

"And you're staying at Frakingham House to research…what exactly are you researching?"

"A neuroscientific hypothesis."

"How curious. What does that entail?"

I was impressed with Mrs. Butterworth's tenacity. Detective Inspector Weeks should employ her to question his suspects. I enjoyed watching Samuel try to avoid answering while remaining polite. It led to a lot of charming smiles in her direction and complicated scientific talk. Her own smile broadened as he spoke, but I was under no illusion that it was due to the mention of lobes and cortexes. Samuel's honey-thick voice and dashing eyes were enough to mesmerize most females. He didn't need to use hypnosis on her.

I caught Jack looking at me and I rolled my eyes. He bit his lip, but it didn't stop his smirk.

"That's nice," Mrs. Butterworth said. "What a clever man

you are, Mr. Gladstone. Your parents must be terribly proud."

"They were," he said.

Mrs. Butterworth didn't seem to notice the past tense. I certainly did, and I also knew that his parents were alive. So why were they no longer proud of their son? "Our son is away at Oxford reading law," the mayor's wife said with a proud thrust of her prominent chin.

"A worthy career. Do you have other children? Daughters perhaps? I saw a little girl looking at us through a window when we arrived."

"That's our ten year-old. We also have twin girls, both seventeen. They're visiting friends this morning. What a shame they're not here. They do like to meet new people, and go to parties and afternoon teas and things. There aren't many in this village worthy to be their friends." Mrs. Butterworth sat up straighter, and I could swear her nose twitched as if she could smell an eligible gentleman. "Not like you and your young friends."

Mr. Butterworth frowned at his wife. "There are several—"

"None of Mr. Gladstone and Mr. Langley's ilk," she said through a hard smile. "They're educated and well-connected, and such charming gentlemen. It is a shame there have been so few opportunities for them to meet Frakingham's newcomers."

This seemed to be aimed directly at Sylvia and Jack and the lack of invitations to Frakingham. Indeed, I began to wonder why the girls hadn't been invited to our dinner party too. Sylvia had only invited older people. The Butterworths, the vicar and his wife, and another couple. Why not people her own age?

"If you'd brought them to church, our daughters could have made their acquaintance," Mrs. Butterworth said pointedly.

"Ah, yes." Sylvia chewed her lip. "The last few weeks have been busy. The vicar understands, as does God, I'm sure."

We refused tea and passed a few more minutes in polite chat with Mrs. Butterworth while her husband seemed to have deflated somewhat and tuned out of the conversation altogether. When finally we made our excuses, he perked up a little and thanked us for stopping by.

We drove back through the village on our way to the vicarage. People stopped to stare and point, something that I was growing used to, but still didn't particularly like. I supposed our visits were infrequent enough that we had become a curiosity. Perhaps the dinner party would put an end to that. I certainly hoped Sylvia was right and that our guests would see how normal we were. That is, how normal we *appeared* to be on the surface. Hopefully August Langley would realize how important the affair was for his niece and be on his best behavior.

The carriage slowed to a stop outside a butcher's shop, nowhere near the vicarage. "What is Olsen doing?" Sylvia asked, peering out the window.

I looked out too and saw another coach just ahead of us. It was a grand, bright red landau with a black top. I'd never seen one like it.

Sylvia pulled the window down and called out to Jack. "Why have we stopped here?"

He hopped down from the driver's seat and approached our window. "They're pointing at us."

"Everyone points at us."

"This is different. The butcher's boy was talking to the driver and pointing along the road out of the village as if he were giving directions. Then he saw us and pointed this way instead. I think the occupants of that landau are on their way to Frakingham to see us."

As he said it, the carriage door opened and a tall gentleman emerged. He held out his hand and a woman's gloved fingers took it. The most elegantly dressed lady I'd ever seen stepped out, followed by another in equally fine attire. Both wore veils over their faces and the perkiest little hats that failed to hide the midnight black of their hair.

"Oh," breathed Sylvia. "*Look* at her coat, Hannah. I adore that shade of peacock blue. Is that braiding across the shoulders? So striking. So modern. Take it all in, so we can sketch them when we get home. I *must* have something similar made up next time we're in London."

Another gentleman alighted behind the ladies. He wasn't as tall as the first and wore glasses, but I could see his beaming smile even at a distance. Indeed, the other gentleman smiled too. I couldn't see if the ladies did or not. The veils covered their entire faces.

Jack opened the door and we piled out as they came up to us. As they drew closer, I could see how handsome the first gentleman was, and how small the two veiled ladies were next to him. It was impossible to tell their age, eye color or whether they were pleased to see us.

"Mr. Langley?" the tall gentleman said, switching his gaze between Jack and Samuel.

"I am Jack Langley," Jack said. "This is Mr. Samuel Gladstone, my cousin Miss Sylvia Langley, and her companion, Miss Hannah Smith."

The gentleman smiled and bowed. "I'm sorry to confront you in the street like this, but the butcher's lad saw your carriage, and we decided we couldn't wait to meet you."

The lady closest to him cleared her throat.

"Forgive me," he said. "I should have introduced myself first. I am Jacob Beaufort. This is my wife, Mrs. Emily Beaufort, her aunt, Miss Cara Moreau, and my brother-in-law, Mr. George Culvert. We're very pleased to meet you, despite the circumstances."

CHAPTER 6

The Frakingham parlor was crowded with the four of us plus Langley and the four from the London party. The parlor in the eastern wing would have seated everyone comfortably, but it was out of bounds until the repairs to the fire-ravaged section were completed. It was fortunate that Langley came with his own chair as there were no more seats to be had.

"We are so pleased you could come," Sylvia said, taking Mrs. Beaufort's hand. "But I must apologize for the state of the house. It's not at its best at the moment."

"There was a fire?" Mr. Beaufort asked.

"Yes. How did you know?"

"The roofline is black in patches."

"How observant of you."

Mr. Beaufort waited, but she did not tell him that I started it, thank goodness. They may be experts on demons and ghosts, but I didn't want them knowing my secret. If Sylvia told them about my fire starting, it would come about that I'd been kept in an attic most of my life, and that wasn't something I wanted known. The Beauforts were much too sophisticated, and I couldn't bear them giving me pitying looks, or worse, curious ones. We'd told them what we'd told

Mr. and Mrs. Butterworth—that I was Sylvia's companion. We left out the part about Yorkshire, and fortunately nobody asked where I was from.

"The house is perfectly lovely, Miss Langley," Miss Moreau said. She sat between Sylvia and me on the settee, her dainty hands folded in her lap.

I'd been shocked when she and Mrs. Beaufort removed their veils. Not only because they were both beautiful with lovely dusky skin and gentle eyes, but because the aunt was younger than her niece. Indeed, Miss Moreau looked to be about my age, while her niece looked a little older. Mrs. Emily Beaufort had explained that her father's sister had just returned from the antipodean colony of Victoria where she'd been living with Mrs. Beaufort's parents. Indeed, all three had come home, although it wasn't clear whether Miss Moreau planned to return with her guardians or remain in England.

"Thank you, Miss Moreau," Sylvia said. "That's most kind of you to say so, but I'm afraid Frakingham has seen better days. It is much brighter now that you and Mrs. Beaufort have arrived. I do adore your outfits. They're very elegant. I fear our old parlor isn't up to receiving visitors like you." She laughed and self-consciously patted her hair.

I caught Mrs. Beaufort looking over their heads at me. She winked, and I was quite taken aback by the intimate gesture. Perhaps she wasn't as formal as she appeared. She was certainly lovely, and I could see why her husband kept casting adoring glances her way. He seemed utterly smitten with her, even eight years after their marriage.

"Do you have any children, Mrs. Beaufort?" I asked.

"Two," she said. "A boy and girl."

"You should have brought them," Sylvia cried. "I adore children."

It was fortunate that they hadn't come. Langley didn't seem like the sort who was fond of children, and the house was at capacity thanks to the repairs.

"It was easier to leave them in London with their nanny

since this is going to be a brief stay. Perhaps another time?"

"Oh, yes, do bring them. Miss Moreau must come again too, and Mr. Culvert and his wife."

"After the baby is born," Mr. Culvert said, his eyes sparkling at the mention of his family. Up until then he'd been quiet, wearing a studious and somewhat bewildered expression, as if he wasn't quite sure how to act around us. "Our second is due in July."

We talked some more until Tommy announced that luncheon was ready.

"What are you doing down here?" I asked him. "I thought you were confined to your room. Our footman was scratched by the demon," I told our guests.

Miss Moreau gasped. "How awful."

Sylvia sniffed. "As you can see, he's quite all right. The best cure for him is to be on his feet and working."

"Miss Langley is right," Tommy said. "I was going numb with boredom. It's good to be down here where I belong."

"What a brave man," Mrs. Beaufort said. "You're very lucky to have him on your staff, Mr. Langley."

Langley grunted a response. "I've had little to do in the way of choosing who works here," he said. "Those decisions seem to get made in my absence."

Once again Mrs. Beaufort looked to me and I simply shook my head. She gave me an understanding smile. I liked her already. Indeed, they were all kind and not at all intimidating as I expected the heir of a viscountcy and his family to be.

Langley left us to dine alone as he always did, and we retreated to the dining room. It wasn't lost on me that everyone seemed more at ease with him gone.

"You must forgive our uncle," Jack said. "He's unused to company."

"I do hope we haven't put him out by coming unannounced," Mrs. Beaufort said.

"Not at all." Jack grinned. "It does him good to have unannounced company once in a while."

"We didn't dare wait another moment," Mr. Culvert said. "Not with a demon on the loose."

"Tell us how you came to know about demons," Jack said.

"I'm a demonologist," Mr. Culvert explained with an air of self-assurance that had been lacking until that point. "My father was one before me. He built up a collection of books on the subject, many of which I've studied over the years."

"You can usually find George with his nose buried in a book in his library," Mrs. Beaufort said with a teasing smile. "It's his favorite place."

"I brought some with me," Mr. Culvert went on. "They're in the landau. Langley, can you describe the demon to me?"

Sylvia groaned in protest.

"Perhaps we shouldn't discuss it at the table," Mrs. Beaufort suggested.

Mr. Culvert frowned. "Why not?"

"George," she scolded.

He pushed his glasses up his nose and shrugged. "Later then, but we shouldn't waste too much time."

"It needn't be a waste," I said. "We'd like to get to know you better."

"Indeed," said Samuel. "Miss Moreau, tell us about Victoria. I cannot imagine living on the bottom of the world."

"Tell me," Sylvia said, "how *does* everyone not fall off?"

Jack gave a wry laugh. "It's called gravity, Syl."

Miss Moreau told us about her life in the city of Melbourne. I was completely fascinated. It was so different to England. I knew instantly that I'd like to visit it one day, until she told me it was hotter there than here.

The conversation eventually came around to Mrs. Beaufort and her aunt's supernatural ability. I admit I'd been skeptical that they could see spirits, but meeting them changed my mind. Both women were far too honest and good to make up stories of that nature and neither profited from their talent anyway.

"So tell us," Samuel said, a mischievous smile on his lips, "can you see any spirits here at Frakingham?"

"Samuel!" Sylvia cried. "Do you *have* to?"

"It's quite all right," Mrs. Beaufort said. "We've encountered none."

"Yet," Miss Moreau added. "Although the ruins we saw on the way in look promising."

That earned her a sharp glare from her niece. When the others fell into conversation around us, I leaned closer to Miss Moreau. "Please tell me if you do see any," I whispered. "I would love to find out more about the people who once lived here."

"Do you think they may be connected to the demon?" she asked, her big brown eyes widening even further.

"Yes and no. If they do have anything to do with the demon, then we all need to know, particularly Mr. Culvert of course, but I'm fascinated by the notion of spirits nevertheless. This place should have one or two. There have been people living on this site for centuries. I would love to take you to the abbey ruins, but it's off limits thanks to the demon."

"You're not appalled by the idea of spirits and mediums?" she asked. "Or frightened?"

"Not at all. I find it interesting." I bit my lip. "I'm sorry. You must think me terribly bad-mannered. I didn't mean to imply you're a curiosity."

Miss Moreau smiled. "I didn't take it that way." She glanced at Sylvia. "I'm not so sure your friend likes dining with spirit mediums, however."

"Don't mind her. She likes things to be easily explained."

"That must make life difficult for her."

I grinned then felt positively awful. Sylvia may not be clever or open-minded, but she was my friend and very sweet. Most of the time.

"Cara," Mrs. Beaufort said, breaking off her conversation with Jack and Samuel, "do you remember the name of the new teacher we employed at the school? I've quite forgotten, and she said she knew Mr. Langley here."

"She did?" I blurted out then bit my lip when everyone looked at me.

Jack's eyes twinkled. Damn him.

"Miss Charity Evans," Miss Moreau said.

The twinkle vanished. He stared at her, and a slight blush infused his cheeks. "Charity," he muttered. He half turned to Tommy, standing by the sideboard, and I got the feeling he wanted to say something to his old friend, but refrained in the company of our guests. They might be kind, but they were nobility and speaking informally to the footman wasn't something people of their class did.

"How did she say she knew me?"

I could see Jack was apprehensive about the answer, but I doubted anyone else noticed. I understood his concern. Just as I didn't want them to know that I'd been kept in an attic, he probably didn't want them to know he'd lived in the alleys of London until the age of fourteen.

"She didn't say," Mrs. Beaufort said. "It only came up because I received your message about the demon when I was visiting the school. Jacob sought me out when it arrived due to its urgent nature. I happened to mention that it was from a Mr. Langley of Frakingham House to Cara who was with me at the time, and Miss Charity overheard."

"She said she used to know you," Miss Moreau said. "The message was from the elder Mr. Langley, but she wasn't to know that."

"I haven't seen her in a year or so," Jack said wistfully. "How is she?"

"I would say she looks well," Mrs. Beaufort said. "She's quite the beauty."

"Indeed," Miss Moreau agreed. "She's very tall and has the loveliest golden hair."

Or course she did. I suppose she also had a sparkling wit, kind nature and no freckles. Jack's eyes had a faraway look in them and a small smile teased his lips. I wondered when he'd last seen her, and what their relationship had been. Certainly not one of mere friendship. He never grew dreamy when he thought of Tommy or any of the orphans he'd left behind when he moved to Frakingham.

"You called her *Miss* Charity," I said, looking down at my plate. I was afraid if I met her gaze she'd realize how important her answer was to me. "I take it she's not wed?"

"No," Mrs. Beaufort said.

"Any beaus?"

"Many, but none she encourages. She's quite married to her work."

"I can't imagine her being a teacher," Jack said, a small smile on his lips. "The Charity I remember was very, uh, spirited."

"She may one day become the headmaster if her devotion to the children and school continue."

"But she's a woman!" Mr. Culvert protested.

"So?"

"The very definition of headmaster is that the position must be held by a man."

"Good lord, George," Mrs. Beaufort huffed. "You can be so ancient in your thinking sometimes. Women are doing all sorts of marvelous things in positions once reserved only for men."

Mr. Beaufort chuckled. "Has being in the company of Adelaide and Emily over the last few years taught you nothing, my friend?"

Mr. Culvert held up his hands in surrender. "I apologize to the ladies present. I can be a little old-fashioned in my thinking at times."

"That's quite all right," I said. "I do agree with you on the point of headmaster. Perhaps she could be called headmistress instead."

We talked some more, thankfully not about Charity's numerous qualities, then adjourned back to the parlor to discuss demons.

"What is a demon exactly?" Samuel asked.

"It's an otherworldly creature," Mr. Culvert explained. "It

has no true form here until it takes over the form of something from this realm."

"I don't understand," I said. "Jack could see it, and Tommy too. Samuel and I could not, nor any of the builders."

Mr. Culvert frowned. "You'd better explain. Tell me the sequence of events."

Jack told him about the hole in the trench, the death of the builder, and how he and Tommy had found the demon again in the woods.

"So Tommy wasn't with you when it first made its presence known?" Mr. Culvert asked.

"No," Jack said.

"Do you think if I had been I wouldn't have seen it either?" Tommy asked.

"Most likely not."

"But I could," Jack said. "Why?"

Mr. Culvert shrugged. "I don't know. All of my research tells me that when a demon comes into this world it has no form. It may be seen as a smoky haze or a ripple of air, but nothing solid."

"We saw the air shudder as it moved," I said.

Samuel nodded. "So you're saying it took on another form between then and later when Tommy saw it in the woods?"

"I see." Jack leaned forward. "It did look different to me that second time too. Remarkably so."

"What did it look like when you first saw it, Mr. Langley?"

Jack described the hairy creature, the claws and a face that was neither human nor animal. I shuddered at the image, thankful that I'd not been able to see it. I would have been terrified out of my wits.

"What about later, in the woods?" Mr. Beaufort prompted. "What did it look like then?"

Tommy and Jack glanced at Sylvia then me. "Why do I get the feeling you're about to say something I won't want to hear?" she asked.

"They avoided answering this question directly at the time," I said to our guests. "Go on, Jack, you'd better tell us now."

"Perhaps the ladies should leave the room," Samuel said.

"Gladly." Sylvia rose. "Come Hannah, Mrs. Beaufort, Miss Moreau. We'll find something more suitable to do."

I could see that Mrs. Beaufort and Miss Moreau weren't too keen to leave and nor was I. "The demon concerns all of us, Sylvia," I said. "We need to listen to what Mr. Culvert has to say about it."

She pouted and sat back down.

Mrs. Beaufort gave Sylvia a comforting smile. "I know it's a disturbing topic, but after what I've seen, I don't frighten easily. You get used to it."

Mr. Beaufort patted her hand, and she turned it over, palm up, and clasped his.

Sylvia picked up her embroidery and tugged hard on the needle. "I doubt I'll ever get used to it. Continue, Tommy. You were about to describe what you saw in the woods."

"I'm not sure I should," he said, watching her. "I don't want to upset you, Miss Langley."

"I'll describe it," Jack said. "Syl is always upset with me so it makes no difference. The demon had changed markedly since the first time I saw it. It walked and ran upright like a human, and it had lost all its fur. It sported skin and the body was definitely that of a human. Of sorts."

"Was it clothed?" Sylvia asked.

"No."

She screwed up her nose. "How awful."

"That's not the awful part. Its face was human, albeit…odd. Like the features didn't fit together. Its nose was too small, its mouth a mere slash, its eyes a strange yellow color, and the face much too big. It was difficult to tell if it was male or female."

"How tall was it?" Mr. Culvert asked.

"About as high as my waist when I'm standing."

Mr. Culvert sat back in his chair and rubbed his chin. "Interesting."

"So what do you think?" Jack asked. "Does it sound like a demon you've seen?"

He blinked. "Oh, no, the thing about demons is that no two look alike. Not when they *become* visible, that is."

"When they become visible?" I asked. "I don't understand. How does it become visible?"

"I don't think George has explained it very well," said Mr. Beaufort patiently, a mischievous sparkle in his eyes. "He has a habit of leaving out important details that he forgets the rest of us aren't aware of."

"I have a lot on my mind," Mr. Culvert said. "Go on, Jacob, you explain it since you think you're an expert now."

"Very well. There are several types of demons, but they don't all become visible to us immediately upon entering our realm. In some cases, it just takes time before it makes an appearance in its true state. For others, it may take exposure to extreme cold or extreme heat. Those types do not change form. They are what they appear to be, neither human nor animal, but something else entirely. That sounds like what you described when you first saw this demon in the trench, Langley. Except yours changed, and that's the other type of demon. Those *do* change form, but usually only once. They may turn into an element—fire or water—or even an inanimate object if they've accidentally consumed one thinking it's sustenance. There is a small but deadly sub-set of the species called shape-shifting demons. They can become multiple things and can change constantly, depending upon what they've consumed."

"Consumed, sustenance," Sylvia echoed, looking a little gray. "I don't think I'm going to like this."

"Probably not," Mrs. Beaufort said with sympathy.

"Most form-changing demons, however, can only alter their appearance once and that change occurs when they first consume the essence of something. The demon then turns into that thing and becomes visible to us in that form. It won't change again, no matter what it attacks."

"When you say consume, do you mean eaten?" Samuel asked.

"In a way," said Mr. Culvert. "Perhaps feasting is a better term. A demon can feast on souls or energy as well as flesh."

"So if it took on the form of the first thing it consumed," Tommy said, frowning, "why didn't it look like the builder? He was the demon's first, uh, meal."

Sylvia pressed a hand to her stomach. "I think I'm going to be sick."

Mr. Culvert shrugged. "I don't know."

"Spirits," I said and everyone looked at me. "You said it can feast on souls, Mr. Culvert. Perhaps the demon consumed something *before* the builder, and that's the form it took and kept. It came from the dungeon," I said to Jack.

"The spirits of the children," he murmured.

Sylvia gave a little cry and dropped her needle. "The deformed Frakingham children. Yes, of course."

We told our guests about the children one of the Lords Frakingham had imprisoned in his dungeon—the same dungeon that had been uncovered during the building repairs and from which the demon had emerged.

"They were said to be imperfect," Jack told them. "Lord Frakingham didn't want the world to know about them so he kept them locked away."

"How awful," Mrs. Beaufort said, tears in her eyes. She seemed far more shocked about that than she did about the demon. "If only I'd known, I could have spoken to them before..."

Her husband put his arm around her shoulders and held her close. She in turn reached for Miss Moreau's hand and when she found it, gave it a squeeze. Both women looked utterly bereft.

To me, the story of the children being locked in the dungeon resonated because of my own situation, but it was still only a story of events that happened a long time ago. The passage of time had lessened the effect on me somewhat. To Mrs. Beaufort and her aunt, however, it must be different. Spirits were real to them, like lost people, and being children must make it so much worse. As mediums, both women helped spirits cross over to the otherworld, but the poor souls of those children might never make it now.

"Mr. Culvert," Tommy said quietly, "are you saying that by the time we saw it in the woods, it had taken on the characteristics of the children from the dungeon?"

"The characteristics of their spirits, yes. Unless we're dealing with a shape-shifting demon, this demon has somehow consumed all the souls of the children together. My guess is that they'd been down there so long, they'd become a single spiritual entity. The demon was able to consume them altogether, but it didn't change form immediately. They don't always. Some do, but others may take a few minutes."

Jack shook his head. "None of this explains why I saw it in the trench when no one else could."

Mr. Culvert looked at his friends and shrugged. "I don't know. I've never known anyone able to see a demon in solid form immediately upon arrival in our realm. Emily, you didn't, did you?"

Mrs. Beaufort shook her head. "I saw a shape-shifting demon many years ago," she told us. "It looked smoky to me until it took on its first human form."

"Let me do some research," Mr. Culvert said. "It's a mystery to solve, and not the only one."

"What is the other?" I asked.

"How did it get into the dungeon in the first place? Was it summoned by someone or did it fall through a portal accidentally, and if so, how was the portal opened?"

"There is another mystery to solve too," Jack said. "How to send it back."

"Or kill it," Tommy said.

"Sending it back will depend on how it got here," Mr. Culvert said. "If it was summoned, then another incantation will banish it. Killing it, on the other hand, is also possible by removing its head with a blade forged in the Otherworld."

"Did you bring one with you?" Sylvia asked.

He chuckled. "Unfortunately I don't have one in my possession here or at home. They're not easily found in this realm. Let me get my books and see what else we can discover about this particular demon."

He fetched his books while Jack sketched what he'd seen. When he returned, Mr. Culvert handed out the books and we paired up to pore over them. Even Tommy leaned over Samuel's shoulder, propriety forgotten. Nobody seemed to care that he'd taken himself off duty, and I suspected I'd been worried all this time for nothing. The Beauforts seemed perfectly at ease with Tommy around.

Jack and I sat very close to one another, but did not touch. When Mr. Culvert handed out the books, it seemed natural that Jack and I would be together. We read in silence, but gradually the temperature surrounding us increased. I could feel heat vibrating off him and my blood began to throb. I moved away and went to sit by the window, as far from the fireplace and the circle of readers as I could get without leaving the room.

He watched me, a troubled frown on his brow, an unspoken question on his lips: *Are you all right?*

I nodded, although I felt quite faint and short of breath. Sweat trickled down the back of my neck into the collar of my dress.

"Miss Smith?" Miss Moreau asked, looking up from her text. "You look quite flushed."

"It's warm in here," I said. "I feel the heat, you see."

Her gaze slid to Jack. "Yes. I see." She smiled knowingly, getting the wrong end of the stick. Well, perhaps not entirely, but my feelings for Jack didn't fully explain why I felt hot.

Part of me wanted to tell her everything, but I held back. She was once more engrossed in her research, and it wasn't a good time. The situation with the demon was urgent and needed their full attention.

They read for a long time, and I rejoined them once I'd

cooled, although I shared the book with Miss Moreau, not Jack. We gave up at dinnertime. No one had found an answer. According to every text, being able to see a demon before it took on its form should be impossible.

I could see that it worried Jack, but he tried not to show it. The dinner conversation remained light, as if we were all avoiding talking or thinking about demons, ghosts and other supernatural phenomena. Mrs. Beaufort even invited us to a ball to be held at their home in honor of Miss Moreau. That put Sylvia in a happy mood, one that had her discussing ball gowns for the remainder of the evening.

The Beaufort party was going to leave early in the morning so retired to their rooms after dinner. Samuel retreated to his room too to work, while Jack and I decided to visit Langley. Sylvia followed and I suspected she was afraid to be left on her own. I couldn't blame her. I was more afraid now that I knew what we were dealing with.

Jack told his uncle everything we'd learned. Langley listened. By the time Jack had finished, his uncle's face had turned pale, the grooves around his mouth tightened.

Langley rubbed his eyes. He looked exhausted. "This is very worrying." He did not look at us as he spoke, but at Bollard.

The servant stood to one side of the door, his hands at his sides. He blinked twice in what I guessed was agreement.

"And this Culvert fellow didn't know why you could see it when no one else could?" Langley asked Jack. "He had no ideas whatsoever?"

"None."

"Then what's the good of him? He shouldn't call himself an expert."

"That's not very fair," I said. "It's not like he's dealing with chemicals and observable reactions." I waved at the scientific paraphernalia crowding his desk. That side of his room was quite a mess with books, papers, tools and storage containers piled on top of each other. Much of his equipment had been destroyed in the fire that ravaged his rooms, but Bollard had salvaged some, and it was all now kept in the same room in which Langley slept.

He glared at me. "There are probably others in the Society For Supernatural Activity who are as knowledgeable as him. I should have asked one of them."

"Why didn't you?"

"I don't have any connections in the Society anymore. I thought Mrs. Beaufort might. It would seem she doesn't."

Sylvia made a sound of protest in the back of her throat. "If you'd spoken more than a few words to her earlier, Uncle, perhaps you would know for sure."

Langley raised both brows at her in surprise. Indeed, I found her little outburst surprising too. "I'm too busy," he said.

"But it's important."

"Let's see what Mr. Culvert can uncover first before we judge him," I said quickly to diffuse the tension between Langley and his niece. "He's going to return to London and consult more texts."

Sylvia pouted. "In the meantime that thing prowls through our woods, stopping us from going anywhere."

"Actually, there are two reasons we can't go anywhere right now," Jack said. "Have you forgotten about Tate?"

"Of course I haven't, but he is after Hannah, not us."

"How comforting," I said tartly.

"I'm sorry, Hannah, really I am." Her face softened and her eyes grew troubled. "I'm just so frustrated. I hate being confined to the house."

"You rarely venture out at this time of year anyway, Syl," Jack said. "Find yourself a nice book and curl up in front of the fire. Have Tommy bring you hot chocolate to soothe your nerves."

She sniffed. "You do say the most ridiculous things."

"If you have all quite finished," Langley interrupted, "would you mind leaving. Bollard and I have work to do."

Jack and I bade him goodnight, but Sylvia did not. She appeared as if she was warring with herself over something.

She chewed her lip until Langley eventually put her out of her misery.

"What is it?" he asked.

"It's just that...you've hardly seen our guests all day."

"And?"

"And Mr. Beaufort is the heir to a viscountcy. He's an important man, Uncle."

"You think I should bow down to my so-called betters, Sylvia? Do *you* think him better than me? Than you or Jack or Hannah?"

"No," she muttered. "Of course not."

He grunted and wheeled himself away from us. "Don't ever let them make you feel inferior. You're not."

"They don't. They're lovely people. If you joined us today, you'd know that."

"I told you, I've been busy in here. I have a lot to do, Sylvia, and little time in which to do it. My work is important."

I could see that she wanted to say more, but in the end, she sighed heavily. "Yes, Uncle. But will you join us tomorrow morning for breakfast? Please. You're the host. You need to be there."

"No, Sylvia, *you* are the hostess. You're old enough now. Jack too." He sounded like an old man too tired to argue anymore. I had to admit, I liked how he was putting more responsibility on her shoulders. Jack was already managing the estate, but she did little more than decorate the house with her pictures and embroidery. She was in a good position as lady of the house. She ought to start taking advantage of it.

"But this is important to me!" She balled her hands into fists and stamped her foot. I'd never seen her speak to her uncle so hotly. "Can't you see that? If I am ever to meet eligible gentlemen, I must associate with respectable people like the Beauforts. Do you want me to remain here and only speak with those who come and go from Freak House? Have you seen how few visitors we get? Probably not because you're always in here with your nose in a beaker and nobody but the automaton for company. Let me tell you, it's not many. Be warned, Uncle, I may end up with a man who is terribly inappropriate."

I glanced at Bollard, but he appeared unmoved at being called an automaton. Langley, however, wheeled himself over to her. "I didn't expect this from you, Sylvia," he said, his voice ice-cold. Did he mean he expected it from me, or Jack? "Do not speak to me again until you've calmed down and found some perspective."

She stormed out the door. I followed, eager to get away. Jack remained behind, which I thought was very brave of him. Sylvia ran off to her room, so I went to my own.

I changed into my nightgown and lay down on the bed with a book. I must have fallen asleep because I awoke to the sound of my door knob turning. It was a clunky old knob like many of the things in this part of the house that hadn't been used until recently, and it creaked loudly.

I sat up and rubbed my eyes. "Jack, is that you? I thought you might want to talk."

The shadowy figure that entered was larger than Jack and moved faster. I recognized the intruder the moment before his big hand clamped over my mouth, stifling my scream.

Ham.

CHAPTER 7

Ham's massive hand clamped tight over my nose and mouth, his other arm wrapped around my waist, squeezing, cutting me in half. A mere flex of muscle would complete the task. I couldn't breathe. Couldn't make a sound.

Didn't he know Tate wanted me alive? Or was he too stupid to realize he was crushing the life out of me?

I struggled, but my flailing arms were quickly pinned to my sides. I bit his palm and nothing but my own bile filled my mouth. He didn't remove his hand. He didn't grunt or hiss in pain.

He dragged me to the door. I struggled all the way, but he simply picked me up, his arm tight around my lower ribs. Tears of pain and panic blinded me, and no matter how much I willed them to stop, they would not.

Think, Hannah.

Fire. I needed the fire.

Nothing happened. I was much too scared to be angry.

Think, think.

I couldn't scream, couldn't hit out with my fists, but my legs were free. He used his foot to flip the door open. I kicked it hard, and it crashed back against the wall. The *bang* reverberated around the room.

Then Jack was there. He seemed to come from nowhere out of the darkness. His fist slammed into Ham's face, stunning the brute long enough for me to wriggle free. I slipped away, and Jack landed more quick punches before Ham recovered.

I'd seen them fight before, but I'd forgotten how strong Ham was. Jack might be fast, but Ham took each blow without pause or care. Most of his return punches missed, but the first to land on Jack's jaw sent him reeling back out to the corridor. He slammed into the wall, and his eyes rolled up into his head.

"Jack!" I screamed.

Doors opened along the corridor. Samuel, Beaufort, and Culvert took in the sight and came to help, although Mr. Culvert was slow as he felt his way along the wall without his glasses. Samuel and Mr. Beaufort grabbed Ham's arms, but he batted them away and went after Jack.

Jack had recovered enough to smash his fist into Ham's nose. Blood sprayed and the oaf fell. Beaufort and Samuel once again took hold of Ham's arms and tried to pin them behind his back, but it was no use. He was too strong. Culvert helped and Tommy too. I hadn't seen him arrive, but the extra man made a difference.

Not enough. Ham wrenched and twisted free. He ran back into my room and headed for the window. Surely he wasn't going to climb out. We were two floors above the ground!

"Stop him!" Jack shouted.

All the men went after him. Jack got to the window first, but Ham had already leapt through it. *Leapt*, not stepped out. He could not have survived the fall.

I closed my eyes. Sick horror flooded me.

"What happened?" Sylvia asked, rushing to my side. She took me in her arms as Miss Moreau and Mrs. Beaufort came up too, each clutching candlesticks. The dancing flames offered enough light to illuminate the room and their shocked faces.

"Bloody hell," Tommy said, looking out the window.

"How did he survive that?" Samuel asked.

Survived? I took Sylvia's hand and joined the men at my window. A shadowy figure ran off down the drive. "Good lord," I muttered.

Jack closed the window, but didn't turn around. He leaned against the sill, his shoulders slumped, his head bowed.

"He's not even limping," I said.

"The fall should have killed him," Sylvia said.

"Yes, it should." Mr. Beaufort adjusted his wife's shawl over her shoulders and put an arm around her to draw her close. She looked up into his eyes, and it was as if they spoke without words. Their love and understanding for one another was truly deep.

"Are you all right, Hannah?" Jack asked. "Did he hurt you?"

"I'm all right." My ribs were a little sore, but I didn't tell him that. He'd only worry.

"Tell us what happened," Samuel said to me. "Did he come in through the window?"

"The door. He gave me no time to scream. He was too fast."

"Not as fast as Mr. Langley," Mr. Culvert said, squinting at Jack. "His movements were a blur."

"That's because you left your glasses in your room," Mrs. Beaufort said. "You know you can't see well without them."

"I could make out enough to know that his speed was incredible."

"He was very fast," Samuel agreed. "I've never seen anyone as fast as that."

Jack merely shrugged. "It's the way I've always been."

Mr. Culvert kept frowning and staring at Jack, but he said nothing more.

"Langley may be fast, but he wasn't as strong as that fellow," Mr. Beaufort said with a nod at the window. "I still can't believe he survived."

"He held off five of us." Mr. Culvert touched the bridge of his nose as if he were pushing up glasses that weren't there. "That's quite a remarkable feat."

"It should never have gotten so far." Sylvia glared at Jack. It took me a moment to realize she was referring to him using his fire. Something he'd said he'd never use on another human being. She knew that, and I thought her accusation a little unfair.

"Are *you* all right, Mr. Langley?" Miss Moreau asked. "He hit you."

A bruise had begun to form under Jack's right eye, but he assured us it didn't hurt. He'd been hit in the stomach and ribs several times too, and must be in pain. "A few bruises are nothing compared to what…" He swallowed hard and glanced at me then quickly away. He swore under his breath.

"Who was he?" Mrs. Beaufort asked. "You all seem to know."

"His name is Ham," I said.

"Is he called that because of the size of his fists?"

"It's short for Hamley. He works for a man named Reuben Tate whom we helped send to prison a few weeks ago. They both escaped and are now coming after us." Nobody corrected me, and the Beaufort party wouldn't have known that Ham had only come for me.

"How awful!" Mrs. Beaufort said.

I heard Langley's wheelchair rolling down the corridor before he and Bollard appeared at the door. Both wore nightcaps, and Langley's smoking jacket appeared to have been hastily thrown on. "What happened?" he said. "We heard shouts and crashes."

"Ham was here," Jack said.

Langley stared at me, the candelabra he held slipping to one side. Sylvia gently prized it off him. He seemed not to be aware of her. His Adam's apple bobbed up and down as he swallowed heavily.

"Hannah's all right," he said, as if someone had asked

him how I was. He cleared his throat and stopped staring. "Good. Very good. Back to bed, everyone. It's late."

"It's early." Mr. Beaufort pointed out the window. Indeed the sun was peeking tiredly over the horizon.

"All the servants have been up for some time," Tommy said. He wore his footman's livery and was the only one of us fully clothed. Everyone else, including the only other servant in the room—Bollard—was dressed in nightclothes.

"Return to your rooms," Langley said to us all. "We'll speak at breakfast."

"But I have a great many questions," Mr. Culvert protested.

Langley looked uncertain, as if he were warring with himself over something. "I imagine you do. But they can wait until breakfast."

"But Mr. Langley—"

Mrs. Beaufort caught her brother-in-law's arm. "Come along, George."

He sighed and left to return to his room. The others also filed out. All except Jack. He stood by the window, his arms crossed over his chest. He was guarding me. My heart swelled and tears sprang to my eyes. I smiled at him and he blinked rapidly back, but there was no responding smile on his lips. I suspected his mood was much too dark for that.

"You too, Jack," Langley said.

"I'm not leaving her."

"Don't make me order you."

"I can't make you do anything, just as you cannot make me. I'm not leaving her, August, and that's final."

Langley wheeled himself across the floor to Jack. "You forget yourself," he said, voice low. "We have guests. What would they think if you remained here alone with Hannah?"

"That I am her protector. They would be correct in their assumption."

"You are also a man, and she a young woman. Leave her alone to dress, and then you can both go down to breakfast."

"No. I won't leave her for even a moment. He might

come back."

"Go, Jack!"

"No." He didn't raise his voice, didn't infuse it with any steel, yet the word was spoken as if his remaining behind was a given. There was no possibility for argument because there was nothing to argue about. It was pure defiance.

"What do you think will happen, Mr. Langley?" I said, throwing my hands in the air. "We can't touch without setting off sparks! Nothing *can* happen. You know that."

Langley sighed. "Neither of you understand," he muttered. Before I could ask him what else there was to understand, he said, "Perhaps Samuel can—"

"No!" Jack growled.

"How would that make any difference?" I asked. "Isn't Samuel's presence in here alone with me as inappropriate as Jack's?"

Langley looked sideways at me, but didn't answer. His suggestion must have been a mistake on his part. He'd probably meant to say Mrs. Beaufort could chaperone while I dressed and her husband also remained to protect me.

What rot. There was no possibility those names could be mixed up, particularly by one of the sharpest minds in England. Surely Langley wasn't trying to push Samuel and me together?

"No one protects Hannah except me," Jack said. "I can save her. If I have to."

By using his fire.

I swallowed the lump in my throat. He'd already made it clear that he didn't want to use his fire on people. He'd once described the smell of burning flesh and the screams, although he'd not told us how and when he'd experienced those things. It sounded horrible, and I didn't want to force him to use his fire on Ham. Knowing that he would if he had to, however, made me feel more secure, albeit only a little bit more. Ham was still out there, as was Tate. My nerves would be on edge until they were locked up again. Or dead.

"Bollard, fetch the maid." Langley turned his chair around and crashed into a table. Bollard stepped forward to help, but Langley waved him off. "I said go!"

Bollard hesitated then left.

"Keep the door open until the maid arrives," Langley said to Jack. "I don't want Hannah's virtue compromised."

"He was willing to compromise it with Samuel," I muttered.

Jack watched him go with a heavy frown. "I don't understand him sometimes."

"I don't understand him ever."

I sat on the bed then flopped onto my back, suddenly utterly exhausted. I was hot too, despite not wearing anything other than a cotton nightdress. I closed my eyes and felt myself drifting to sleep.

"Hannah?"

I opened them again to see Jack standing by my bed. He sat down beside me, close but not touching. "Are you sure you're all right?"

"I'm a little shaken," I admitted. "And tired."

"Rest for a while. I'll be here when you wake up." It was the nicest, kindest thing he could have said at that moment.

I closed my eyes and fell asleep.

***

He was indeed still there when I awoke. He lay beside me on his back, his hands clasped over his stomach. When I stirred, he sat up.

"Feeling better?" he asked.

"A little warm."

"Sorry." He got off the bed and went to the window. That's when I noticed Maud sitting in the armchair, mending one of Sylvia's jackets. Our chaperone.

Weak morning light chased away the shadows in the room and outside, clouds hung low. "How long have I been asleep?" I asked.

"An hour," Jack said. "You've had three visitors, all of whom I sent away." He was dressed in trousers and shirt, so

I suspected one of those visitors had been Tommy with clothes. "Are you ready for breakfast?"

I got up and opened my wardrobe doors. I selected a dress, but not a jacket. Next I needed unmentionables. I bit my lip and glanced at Jack.

He lifted an eyebrow. "Everything all right?"

I twirled my finger. "Face the other way, please."

He blushed and dutifully turned to look out the window. I selected what I needed and Maud helped me dress. "Mr. and Mrs. Beaufort are lovely people," I said, making idle conversation. There was very little we could talk about with Maud in the room.

"Hmmm," Jack said.

I lifted my arms and Maud placed the corset around me. "I like Miss Moreau too."

"Yes." The word was a hiss from his lips.

"Mr. Culvert is a little odder than the others, but that could be because of his profession." A profession that I would not name in front of Maud.

When Jack didn't answer, I glanced over my shoulder at him. Our gazes connected in the reflection of the window glass. He'd been watching me the entire time. It was impossible to tell if he blushed, but his eyes widened upon being caught and he turned away quickly. My own face blazed like a torch.

Maud finished with the corset and fetched my dress from the bed. It gave me the opportunity to look at Jack again. His forehead rested on the window frame, and he gripped the sill with one hand.

I put on my dress with Maud's help and sat at my dressing table so she could do my hair. "You may turn around now, Jack."

He sat on the bed, and I watched him in the mirror's reflection, but this time he didn't seem to notice me looking. He was too intent on the back of my neck and hair. His eyes followed every movement of Maud's fingers as she pinned the curls high on my head. I recognized the hungry desire in his gaze, and felt it within myself, throbbing like a primal drumbeat. I loved how he watched me like that, with an intensity that made me feel like I was the most important thing in his world, that we were the only two people in the room. That nothing else mattered and everything would be all right.

My hair finished, Maud fixed a black ribbon around my throat. Jack licked his top lip and a bead of sweat trickled down his hairline.

"There," Maud said. "What do you think, Mr. Langley, sir?"

"She's beautiful," he murmured. His gaze finally connected with mine in the mirror. "Absolutely beautiful."

Not being able to touch him was awful. Until now. Now, it felt devastating. I ached to reach for him, kiss him, and feel his arms around me.

Maud cleared her throat. "Ready, Miss Smith?"

"Hmmm?"

"For breakfast."

"Yes. Of course." I tore my gaze away from Jack, but as I left the room, I could feel him still watching me. We walked down the corridor a little behind Maud, so she couldn't overhear us as we whispered.

"I'm sorry about my behavior earlier," Jack said. "I didn't meant to watch you."

"It's quite all right."

"No, it's not. But in my defense, a man can only be gentlemanly to a point."

I laughed. "Stop worrying. There was no harm done."

"Speak for yourself," he muttered. "I think I turned around too soon."

"Nonsense. There was only my hair left to do."

"I know. I found the event rather…" He coughed. "Nice."

"Nice?"

"Very well, not nice. Alluring. Enthralling." His voice had become velvet thick and deep, rumbling across the space between us and rolling over me. I could listen to him whisper words like that in my ear all day. I longed for it.

Maud turned a corner up ahead, and Jack stepped in front of me. Heat surrounded us and I felt like we were in a bubble, safe and together. He leaned closer, his mouth an inch from mine. His hooded gaze focused on me, searched my face, taking in every freckle.

"Hannah," he murmured.

One small movement and we would be kissing. That's all it would take. I wanted to. God, how I *needed* to.

"I want to unpin your hair," he went on, "and let it slide through my fingers. I want to kiss the nape of your neck, the hollow at your throat, your shoulder. I want to trace the curve of your spine, the flare of your hip. Slowly. So very, very slowly."

My skin tingled. My heart pulsed at every image he conjured with his soft, urgent words. It was as if he were doing all those things to me right there in the corridor with Maud just around the corner.

I felt like I was going to explode with the heat flowing through me. But I didn't care. I wanted to hear more. Wanted to feel his words sliding over me like melted chocolate.

"And then?" I murmured, my lips so close to his I could almost taste him.

"Then I'll kiss the arch of your foot, your ankle, and work up to your knee. I want to worship every inch of you. When you're quivering in my arms, I'll—"

"Miss Smith?"

We leapt apart as Maud peered round the corner. Her narrowed gaze left no doubt that she knew what we'd been doing. Or almost doing.

I followed her without looking at Jack as I passed him, although I could feel his heat and hear his ragged breathing. My nerves didn't stop tingling until we reached the dining room where breakfast was already underway. Everyone was there, including Langley. The conversations ceased as we entered.

"I fell asleep," I said.

Langley's gaze slid past me to Maud. There was no exchange of words between them, but I got the feeling something was conveyed before he dismissed her with a nod. Bollard was the only servant remaining since he was there to serve Langley. Everyone else served themselves from the selection of dishes on the sideboard.

"We were just going over the events of this morning," Mr. Beaufort said.

"I thought as much," I said, picking up a plate.

Mrs. Beaufort winced. "Was it that obvious?"

I smiled at her. "It's natural to want to talk about it. Don't stop on my account."

"What have you told them?" Jack asked his uncle.

"That Tate wants Hannah, and Hannah only."

"He also told us why," Mr. Beaufort said.

Mr. Culvert scrunched up his napkin and placed it on the table. "I must say, you kept that secret well. I wouldn't have known you were a, er, whatever it is you want to call yourself."

"Fire starter," I said with a shrug.

"We're considering naming the condition autoflamma," Sylvia said, her teacup paused at her lips. "That would make her an autoflammian I suppose."

"You can't mix the Greek and Latin," Mr. Culvert protested. He looked quite shocked at the thought. "What about egoflamma. Ego means self in Latin."

Sylvia screwed up her nose. "I don't particularly like the sound of it."

"I'm throwing my money behind something with neuro in it," Samuel said.

"You would say that."

Mr. Culvert's next comment was cut off by Mrs. Beaufort. "Perhaps we can leave the naming of her talent to another time."

"Talent?" I scoffed. "Hardly. Did Mr. Langley tell you I

only do it when I'm angry? It's not a talent unless you can control it." There. That should put an end to such nonsense. There was no need to glorify it. "Like Jack can."

The room went quiet. Cutlery stilled. Sausages and eggs were forgotten. It would seem Jack hadn't been mentioned at all, only me. I looked to Langley for explanation, but received a frosty glare for my troubles. Why didn't he want them to know about Jack?

"Interesting," Mr. Culvert said, staring at Jack. "Tell me about it, if you don't mind."

Jack set his plate down on the table and sat. "There's nothing much to tell. I can start fires at will, Hannah can't, nor can Tate. It's something I've always been able to do."

"Why?" Mr. Beaufort asked.

Mr. Culvert leaned forward over his plate, smearing bacon grease on his jacket. "Yes, why?"

Jack shrugged. "Nobody knows."

Both Mr. and Mrs. Beaufort looked to Langley. He sat in his wheelchair, quietly chewing, and either didn't notice or pretended not to.

Mr. Culvert didn't notice either. "Is it connected to your speed?" he asked.

Jack slowly looked up from his plate. "Pardon?"

"Your speed. When you fought that man this morning, you were very fast."

"I suppose I'm a little faster than others."

"I can assure you," Culvert said, "you were much faster than the average man."

"Agreed," Samuel said.

Jack *was* incredibly fast and not just when he was throwing punches. I'd seen him exercising on the banks of the lake. He'd run between trees, reaching them in remarkably quick time. And when he swam, he could glide through the water like a fish.

Surely those skills were not connected to the fire?

Jack appeared quite shocked by Mr. Culvert's observation. His food sat forgotten, his knife and fork lay idle. Everyone stared at him. Everyone except Langley and Miss Moreau. She was watching me.

"Miss Smith?" she prompted. "Is there something else?"

I looked down at my plate. "Nothing."

"It's all right, Hannah," Jack said. "I want to hear what you have to say too."

I swallowed and told them about his exercising and swimming. When I'd finished, he merely shrugged. "Those things are not out of the ordinary. Not like the fire starting."

"Don't be so certain," Mr. Culvert said. "If Miss Smith has observed your unnatural speed too, perhaps it's something we need to investigate further."

"Why?" Sylvia asked.

"Because it may be linked to his fire in some way. It's certainly an angle worth pursuing."

"An angle? I don't understand. Are you going to study my cousin?"

"I wouldn't put it quite like that, no. I'm intrigued by him, that's all. Don't you want to know why you're like this, Mr. Langley?"

"Yes," Jack said.

"You see, Miss Langley, where Miss Smith can't control her fires, your cousin can. I suspect he was born with that ability as well as others. It seems too coincidental that he possesses a number of other supernatural characteristics. There must be a connection."

"Yet it may just be coincidence," Jack said.

Mr. Culvert conceded the point with a nod. "In any type of scientific-based research, coincidences are seen as potential clues to a single underlying source. When an unlikely coincidence is discovered, we tend to follow it to see where it leads."

"You consider yourself a scientist?" Samuel asked.

"Of course. A lot of my research is done through texts, however. I rarely have the opportunity to study those who possess supernatural abilities in person."

"But you're a demonologist," I said.

"I've branched out in recent years to include supernatural phenomena."

"Isn't that what the Society For Supernatural Activity does?"

"You know about them?" Mr. Beaufort asked.

"Uncle used to be a member," Sylvia said. "Tate too."

The Beauforts and Mr. Culvert turned to him as one. "I let my membership lapse some years ago," Langley said.

"I operate independently of them," Mr. Culvert said. "My research is mostly informal and done in my spare time."

"So you think Jack worth studying?" Sylvia asked.

"Absolutely."

She shivered. "You're frightening me, Mr. Culvert."

"George has a habit of doing that," Mrs. Beaufort said with a scowl at her brother-in-law. "Be assured, he doesn't intend to bring harm to your cousin."

"Tell me about your parents," Mr. Culvert said to Jack. "Were they like you?"

Jack shrugged. "I don't know. They died when I was young."

Mr. Culvert looked to August Langley. "Can you shed some light on his—"

"No," Langley said. "I cannot help you there. Much of his early background is unknown. Now, may we end the conversation?"

"Of course," Mr. Beaufort said with a glance at his brother-in-law.

Mr. Culvert's face fell. "But—"

"George!" Mrs. Beaufort snapped.

He sighed. "May I bring up an unrelated observation instead?"

"Of course," Langley said.

"That intruder this morning was remarkably strong. Too strong for a normal man."

"I thought you said it was unrelated," Mr. Beaufort said dryly.

"It is. Unrelated to Mr. Jack Langley. Of course, it's just

an observation and now that the brute is gone, I can't study him further. Do any of you know more about him?"

"He's just a hired man of Tate's," Sylvia said.

"So we believed," I said. "Could he be..." I hesitated, not sure I wanted to voice my thought. "Could he be the result of one of Tate's experiments?" I looked to Langley as I said it.

"I don't know," he said. "What Reuben Tate has done in the intervening years since I last saw him is a mystery to me. I don't know his man's background."

But did he know Jack's? I could see the same question churning through Jack's mind too as he stared at his uncle. He'd been remarkably quiet when Langley claimed not to know anything about his parents. I wondered if he was thinking what I was thinking—how could a man not know whether his brother had freakish abilities, or his brother's wife?

Or did Jack, like me, suspect that August Langley wasn't really his uncle? Whether or not he was, Langley had known Jack as a baby. He'd already admitted as much. Somehow they'd lost touch until eight years ago when Langley had found Jack in London. He must know more than he was letting on.

"I wonder," Mr. Culvert said, picking up his knife and fork.

"Wonder what?" Miss Moreau asked.

"Whether Ham's a demon."

CHAPTER 8

Sylvia was the first to make a sound; however, her wild laughter was quite out of place. The rest of us were stunned into silence.

"Mr. Culvert," she said, "you do say the most absurd things." Her laughter faded when she saw that nobody else joined in.

"If he were a demon," Samuel said, "wouldn't he have…consumed one of us?"

"Only if he were hungry," Mr. Culvert said.

Sylvia put her napkin to her mouth and stifled a cry.

"Tate may be feeding him," Culvert went on. "In which case Ham doesn't need extra sustenance."

"What would Tate feed him?" Sylvia asked.

"Animals, birds…"

"Ugh."

Mr. Beaufort nodded, thoughtful. "Tate must be controlling it, telling it what to do."

"We've come across this before," Mr. Culvert said. "Somehow Tate has found a way to summon a demon and control it. The first thing it must have consumed when it arrived in this realm was a man of Ham's likeness."

"That's why it looks so human," Mrs. Beaufort said.

Sylvia gave another cry and fled the room entirely. Nobody went after her. I was much too fascinated by what our guests were saying not to hear more.

"It explains why Ham is so strong," Samuel said. "And how they escaped prison. I knew there had to be another explanation."

"So," Mr. Langley cut in. "We have two demons on the loose."

Quiet descended again as that piece of information sank in.

Nobody ate much after that. Langley returned to his room and the Beaufort party prepared to leave. We met them again twenty minutes later in the entrance hall to say our goodbyes.

"This visit has been much too short," Mrs. Beaufort said, hooking her arm through mine.

Miss Moreau took my other arm. "We've enjoyed meeting you all immensely."

"And we you," I said. "Thank you for your assistance this morning. I'm sorry you were embroiled in our troubles."

"I'm glad we were here to help," Mr. Beaufort said with a bow.

Mr. Culvert agreed. "I can't imagine how you fought Ham off the last time, Langley."

Jack merely shrugged. "The fire helped."

"And your speed?"

"That too."

"Thank you for the information about demons," Samuel said. "It's been an invaluable lesson. Hopefully we can use some of that knowledge to remove it."

"I'll do more research at home and write out an incantation to send the rogue demon back, but in the mean time you must do something for me."

"What is that?" Langley asked.

"Investigate the dungeon. Find out how it came to be here. Are there any signs of supernatural activity down there?

An amulet or something otherwordly that could have been used to summon it perhaps?"

"Is that important to send it back?" Sylvia asked, hugging herself. I admired her for staying put and not running off this time.

"It may be," Culvert said. "If it were summoned from this side, then a simple incantation said in its presence and that of the amulet will return it."

Her eyes widened. "Somebody brought it here?" she asked, echoing my own thoughts.

"Tate perhaps," I offered.

Jack's gaze locked with mine. "I would say it's quite likely."

"Let's not jump to conclusions," Mr. Culvert said. "On occasion, demons have appeared in this realm with no one taking claim for summoning it. I believe they've been sent from their own realm for a purpose."

"Surely not," Samuel said.

Mr. Culvert pushed his glasses up his nose. "It's a possibility. It's also possible that no one owns up to summoning it because they're afraid of the repercussions. I can't be sure, so I keep an open mind."

"Very commendable."

We said more goodbyes at the door. Tommy handed out coats, hats and gloves, then Jack escorted the Beauforts to the waiting carriage. The landau had been equipped with torches tied to the coach lamps. They blazed brightly in the hazy morning light. Hopefully they wouldn't encounter any demons since they weren't traveling near the woods, but it was best to be careful.

Jack returned and escorted Miss Moreau out then came back for Mr. Culvert.

"If you learn anything more about this Ham creature, let me know. And about yourself too," Mr. Culvert said to Jack.

As they walked down the steps, I could see Jack ask him something and then they both stopped suddenly. Mr. Culvert spoke, but I couldn't hear his words. There was a lot of head shaking and shrugging, then he shook Jack's hand before climbing into the carriage.

Jack waved them off and returned inside and shut the door.

"Well?" Langley said.

"Well what?"

"What did you ask him?" Sylvia prompted. "You know, you should have just asked him in front of us. It would save repeating it."

"I didn't ask in front of you because I wasn't sure I wanted you to hear the answer."

"And now?" Samuel asked.

"You don't have to tell us anything, Jack," I said.

Sylvia snorted softly. "He most certainly does. We are all stuck here together with two demons running about and a madman controlling one of them. What else could be said that would make things worse?"

"It's all right," Jack said to me. "He didn't say anything too alarming."

"Well?" Langley said again. "What did you ask him?"

"I wanted to know if he thought I was a demon."

"A what!" Sylvia spluttered. "Don't be absurd. Of course you're not. What gave you that idea?"

"Ham, my abilities. If it was just the fire starting, I would have thought nothing of it, but as you all pointed out, there's the speed too, and the swimming."

"What did he say?" I asked, my chest tightening. My hands felt hot and I blew on the palms to cool them. It didn't help.

Sylvia took a step away from Jack, but eyed him closely.

"He doesn't think I'm a demon," he said.

She breathed a sigh. "Thank goodness. Of course, we knew you weren't. It was an absurd notion."

"I needed to hear an expert's opinion."

"What explanation did he give for coming to his conclusion?" Langley asked.

I didn't point out that Jack had claimed Culvert only

thought he wasn't a demon. That wasn't a conclusion. I was surprised Langley overlooked the distinction since he was a scientist. I too decided to dismiss it, however. Jack was most certainly not like Ham or that creature.

Then again, he wasn't like us either.

"For one thing, I'm too human," he said. "I behave and speak like a human. I have my own will and desires." He glanced at me. "I assured him they were very human in nature too."

"Anything else?" Langley snapped.

"He doesn't think I'm strong enough. Demon strength is unnatural, he said. Like Ham's. He's not seen any evidence to the contrary."

"That's comforting," Sylvia offered.

Not really, but I didn't tell her that it meant Jack couldn't fight either Ham or the other demon on his own. He would almost certainly lose if pitted in battle against either for any length of time. Thank goodness for his fireballs. Perhaps now that he knew Ham wasn't human, he wouldn't hesitate to use them if attacked.

"I have work to do," Langley said. Bollard stepped forward to wheel him away, but Jack intervened.

"Who are my parents?" he asked casually.

Langley sighed. "We've spoken about this. I can't answer you."

Can't or won't? "I thought you and Jack's father were brothers," I said.

"Yes," Jack said quietly, not taking his eyes off his uncle. "That's what he'd have everyone believe."

Bollard wheeled Langley away. The four of us watched him go.

Jack heaved a great sigh that seemed to deflate him. He looked exhausted. "It's always the same response. I'm growing tired of his evasion."

"You think he's lying?" Samuel asked.

Jack shrugged. "I don't know, but he's never satisfactorily answered my questions about my father or told me how he came to find me in London."

"Yet you came to live here with him anyway," I said. "Why, when you had doubts?"

"Would you want to live here if your home was a derelict house and you were always hungry?"

"You're right, I'm sorry." I bit my lip, wishing I could take it back.

"It's all right, Hannah," he said gently. "I came here because it was a way out of London and that life. The only way. I don't regret it. I do regret not asking more questions back then. He may have been more willing to give them if I'd refused to come with him. Now he probably doesn't see the need. I don't mind telling you that I was afraid he'd throw me out if I questioned him too much."

"Are you still afraid of that?"

It was a long time before he answered me. "This is my home, my family. Before today, I didn't want to jeopardize it over something that essentially changed nothing. Now, my need to know has grown."

"Then why not go and pester him until he answers?" Sylvia said.

"Because being thrown out means leaving Hannah here, and you. He's your guardian, and Wade is Hannah's. I can't take either of you with me until you're twenty-one."

"What have you already asked him about your father?" Samuel asked.

"What was he like? Was he older or younger than August? What were their parents like? Could anyone else in the family do this?" He looked down at his hands, turning them over to look at the backs as well as the palms.

"It can't be from your father," Sylvia said. "Or I'd be able to do it too, and Uncle."

She'd missed the point entirely. Jack doubted he was even related to her and Langley. I had strong doubts too. There seemed to be no reason for Langley to be so tight-lipped about it, unless it was all a lie.

"It's frustrating to think he may have answers and is

refusing to tell me," Jack said.

"I'm sure he'd tell you if it were important," Sylvia said.

"It's important to me!"

She swept her hands in an arc to encompass the entrance hall where we stood with its high ceiling, grand staircase and arched doors leading to a maze of corridors and rooms. "You said it yourself. You cannot risk losing all this by asking questions about people who have had very little bearing on your life."

I failed to see how parents could have very little bearing on one's life since they were the ones who'd given that life, but I didn't say anything. Jack was clearly frustrated, and she was obviously disinterested. I couldn't see them ever agreeing.

"At least we now know what we must contend with in Ham," I said, changing the subject.

Samuel seemed relieved to have the subject changed too. He leapt on the new topic eagerly. "It's certainly better than not knowing."

Sylvia shuddered. "How can we defeat a demon? *Two* demons! We have no special sword, incantation or amulet. Not even the so-called expert could help us."

"Be fair, Syl," Jack said. "Culvert did say the incantation depends on how Ham came to be here. We know that Tate probably summoned Ham, but as for the other demon, we must find out how it arrived in our realm. I'll investigate the trench."

"Alone?" Tommy asked. He'd been standing quietly to one side, listening to our conversation but not interfering.

Jack headed for the door. "You're not coming."

"But—"

"No! We've been through this." He opened the door and was gone before any of us could urge him to be careful.

Tommy stormed off in the direction of the service area, clearly irritated at being left out.

Sylvia watched him go, sighed, then turned to me. "What shall we do today, Hannah? Would you like to embroider together?"

I'd rather spend the morning facing down a demon. "I think I'll rummage through the attic some more."

"Good idea," Samuel said. "I'll meet you up there." He headed up the stairs, taking two at a time.

Sylvia watched him go and sniffed. "Why bother? We already had a thorough look and found nothing. Besides, Mr. Culvert didn't say anything about understanding the spirits of the children, only that we must learn how the demon came to be here."

"Nevertheless, it makes me feel useful. I cannot sit and do nothing."

"Embroidery is not nothing, Hannah. Nor is painting or sketching or— I've just had a thought! Why don't we sketch Miss Moreau's and Mrs. Beaufort's outfits? We can give them to our dressmaker when next we're in London."

"You're such a wonderful artist, Sylvia, why don't you do it? I couldn't possibly do justice to the designs with my lack of skill."

"You have a point."

I didn't know whether to laugh that my flattery had worked or be offended.

We went our separate ways, but instead of heading to the attic, I instead went in search of Tommy. I found him in the small room off the kitchen where the silver was kept in locked cabinets. The doors of one cabinet were flung open, displaying the impressive array of silver plate, candlesticks, and tea services. Tommy sat at the square central table wearing white gloves. He was rubbing a spot on a teapot with a cloth over and over as if it wouldn't come clean. It looked shiny enough to me.

"Careful," I said, "you'll make Aladdin's genie appear, and we have quite enough supernatural creatures on our hands thank you."

He paused and inspected his handiwork. "Wasn't the genie confined to a lamp?" With a sigh, he put the teapot down and picked up a platter. "Is there something I can do for you, Miss Smith?"

"Tommy, please call me Hannah when we're alone together."

"No."

"You're as stubborn as he is, you know."

"Which Mr. Langley are you referring to?" He dabbed some of the silver cleaner onto his rag and smeared it over the platter.

"The description fits them both, but I was referring to Jack."

Tommy's rubbing got harder. "He shouldn't have gone out by himself."

I sat on the chair beside him and put my hand over his, stilling it. He looked at me. "Tommy, you can't go with him this time. You're injured and he was right. He can't use the fire if you're in trouble. He can't risk hurting you."

"Doesn't make it any easier to sit here doing nothing while he's out there." He snatched his hand away and threw the rag on the table.

"I know."

He looked at me and frowned. "Sorry, ma'am, it can't be easy for you either."

"Like you, I've decided to keep busy while he's off investigating the trench." I picked up the rag and the platter and began polishing.

He chuckled. "You must want to ask me something."

"Is it that obvious?"

He took back the rag and the platter. "You need gloves, and you're doing it wrong anyway."

"There's a technique to this?"

"Of course. Do you want me to show you, or do you want to ask me what you came down here to ask?"

"You're much too perceptive, Tommy."

"We footmen have to be." He winked. "We have to know what our masters and mistresses want before they do themselves."

"Is that so? In that case, what have I come to ask you?"

"Something about Jack."

I sighed. "I really am obvious, aren't I?"

"Only where Jack's concerned. Go on then. Out with it."

"I want to know why he doesn't like to use his fireballs on people, not even to save himself."

"Ah." He returned to polishing the platter, circling the rag around the rim slowly, thoughtfully. "Why don't you ask him?"

"Because I suspect he won't tell me."

"Then it's not my place to tell you either."

I sighed. "As frustrating as it is, I admire your loyalty."

He went to pick up the bottle of silver polish, but I snatched it away. "Miss Smith, pass me the bottle please."

I held it behind my back.

He gave me a lopsided grin. "I won't tell you, no matter how many times you ask or what games you play."

"I have a different question then."

"You ask a lot of questions."

"So I've been told."

He tapped his gloved fingers on the table. "You'd better go on before Mrs. Moore comes in. She doesn't like me talking to the ladies of the house."

"Tell me about Miss Charity Evans."

His smile started slowly at one corner of his mouth and spread to the other. "Ah. Her."

"Who is she and how does Jack know her? And this time, don't tell me it's not my place to ask."

"You've got naught to worry about, Miss Smith."

"Who said I was worried?"

I handed him the bottle of polish, but he set it and the rag down on the table. "Very well, you want to know about Miss Charity, I'll tell you. She grew up with us in London."

"She was an orphan?"

He nodded. "She joined us when we were aged about nine. Jack found her shivering on a street corner one winter. She wore no shoes, no coat, and no one was buying the matches she was trying to sell. She was half dead. He took

123

her back to our place—"

"*Your* place?"

"We lived in an abandoned house. It was an old building, almost falling down around us. Some of the beams had broken and rotted away, floorboards and entire walls were missing. I'm sure it was held together with nothing more than cobwebs and dust. But it had a roof and that's all we needed with Jack's fire to keep us warm. He brought Charity home and we fed her as best we could with what food we could find. Like all the others, she never left."

"Was she a...particular friend of Jack's?"

He gave me that grin again. I was finding it quite irritating. "Of sorts."

"What does that mean?"

He chuckled. I didn't know what he found so amusing. He probably suspected I was jealous. He was right.

His smile faded as the gaze in his eyes grew distant. "They was fond of each uvver," he said, slipping into the London accent I'd heard him use only with Jack. "She were a match for Jackie, though. They both had terrible tempers back in them days and would rail at each uvver over nuffing. What I thought was nuffing, anyways. After the flare ups, they wouldn't talk for days sometimes, but then somefing would happen and they'd all be friendly again, if you know what I mean."

Unfortunately, I did. "At fourteen? Isn't that a little young to be...getting friendly?"

My question seemed to shock him out of his reverie and his accent. "I, uh, suppose so." He blushed fiercely. "But you've got to remember that we lived differently. Our world had few rules. What wasn't acceptable for the rest of society was perfectly all right to us. There were no manners or etiquette, and no adults to teach us proper behavior." He grew redder and redder and eventually returned to polishing the platter, too embarrassed to look at me.

"Did Charity fall pregnant?" I asked.

He shook his head. "No, thank God. It would have been

a terrible place to bring up a baby, and she was too young to be a parent. Jack too."

I blew out a breath. That was something at least. "So how did they part? Did it happen when Jack came here with Langley?"

"They parted a month or so before."

"Why?"

"Don't know if I should say, ma'am."

"Tommy!"

"It's not my place, Miss Smith."

I sighed. "Does it have anything to do with Jack's fire starting?"

His polishing slowed, and I got the feeling I'd guessed right. "You'd better ask him that."

"I will. He mentioned that he'd seen her just a year ago, and the orphans who came here recently mentioned her too. I got the impression she'd been helping them."

"She was, along with Patrick before Tate killed him. We saw her from time to time when we went to London to check on them, but she left there a while ago."

Patrick had been killed by Tate to keep him silent. Unfortunately he'd been the only adult taking care of the group of orphans, using Langley's money to support them. With him gone, and the elusive Miss Charity no longer around, the school under Mrs. Beaufort's patronage had taken them in.

"Now she's turned up at Mrs. Beaufort's school," I said. "I find that quite a coincidence."

Tommy shrugged. "Jack doesn't think she'd make a good teacher, but I do. She understands orphans and children. Mind you, she might have trouble staying in the one place long enough."

"She travels a lot?"

"She goes from place to place."

"Is that why she and Jack parted company?"

Another shrug. More evasion.

"I'll ask Jack that too, shall I?"

He stopped polishing altogether. "Be careful, Miss Smith. Don't open up old wounds. Jack and Charity were…well, they were hot and cold. When they were happy, they were very happy, but they could make each other miserable too, and those around them."

Yes, but were they *finished?*

It's the question that had eaten at me ever since Mrs. Beaufort had mentioned Charity's name. The look that had come over Jack had been one of fondness. Clearly he remembered the good times and not the bad. Perhaps it had never been as awful as Tommy remembered. Perhaps he'd been jealous of his friend's affections for the girl and that had colored his perception.

Either way, the gnawing in my gut would not go away.

"Tommy," I said, pulling my chair closer. I pressed my hand over the rag to stop the polishing. He looked at me, one eyebrow raised. "Tommy, does Jack's reluctance to use fireballs on people have anything to do with Charity?"

His lips parted and a soft huff of breath escaped. "Miss Smith—"

"Hannah, there you— Tommy!"

I spun round to see Sylvia standing in the doorway, glaring at me. Or not at me, but at the rag that both Tommy and I held, our fingers almost touching. I let it go.

Tommy bent over the platter and put all his concentration into polishing the silver. He didn't look at either of us.

"Hello, Sylvia," I said. "What are you doing here?"

"I could ask you the same question."

"I came to ask Tommy something about Jack."

She narrowed her eyes. "Did you come to help polish the silver too?"

"I—"

"Tommy," she said sharply.

He stopped polishing and stood to attention, but kept his head bowed. Poor Tommy. He didn't deserve to be shamed in front of me. Sylvia was being quite horrible to him.

"Yes, Miss Langley? What can I do for you?" he asked.

"You can bring up some tea."

"Yes, ma'am. Right after I lock the silver away."

"Leave the silver. Who's going to steal it?"

"But—"

"Tommy. My tea."

He gave a curt bow and headed into the adjoining kitchen.

Sylvia spun on her heel and walked off. I ran after her and hooked my arm through hers. She tried to unlink herself, but I held on tight. "Why didn't you simply ring for him? Was it necessary to come all the way down just to ask for tea?"

"Clearly it was." She held her nose so high in the air, she was in danger of giving herself a sore neck. "If I hadn't, who knows what might have happened?"

"Sylvia! You don't believe that, do you?"

She paused at the bottom of the stairs and sighed. "I don't know what to think."

"Then let me tell you. Don't think *that* because you'd be quite wrong. I was asking Tommy about Charity, and how she and Jack knew one another. There is nothing untoward happening between Tommy and me."

The lines around her mouth and forehead smoothed. "I only worry about you, Hannah. I know you don't understand all the intricacies of a gentlewoman's relationship with the staff, and as your friend, it falls to me to teach you."

"You're too kind," I said, crisp.

"I am trying, Hannah. Really I am." We slowly ascended the stairs together, our arms still linked. "You may not realize how terrible it would be for you and a footman to have relations, but believe me it would be the single worst mistake of your life."

"That bad?"

"Oh yes. Uncle would throw you out, then he'd fire Tommy without a reference. He'd never work in service again."

When she put it like that, it would indeed be a terrible thing. Tommy wasn't qualified for any other job. He had no experience other than as a footman.

"I believe you when you say you have no interest in Tommy in that way," she said, "but only because I've seen how you look at Jack."

How did I look at Jack?

"Uncle may not be quite so understanding," she went on. "He certainly wants no familiarity of any kind between us and the servants. He doesn't even like Jack and Tommy being friends, so they pretend otherwise when they're in Uncle's company."

"Yet he's always telling you not to think of yourselves as being of lesser value than others. I thought he was quite egalitarian."

"Perhaps only in theory."

Or perhaps only when it worked in his favor. He may consider himself and his family equal to Lord Wade for example, but those lower on the social ladder could not, and should not, think of themselves as higher.

"I see," I said. "Thank you for the warning, Sylvia. I'll be more careful next time."

"No! There will be no next time. Understand? Now, let's prop ourselves at a window where we can see the trench. Jack may not want anyone to go with him, but we can keep watch anyway."

I liked her idea so settled beside her on the window seat in her bedroom. If we angled ourselves just right, we could see the trench. We were only there a few minutes when Jack emerged and made his way not to the house, but to the lake.

"What's he doing?" Sylvia asked.

"Going for a swim," I said.

Jack did indeed remove his shoes and waistcoat and walk into the shallows. When he was thigh-deep, he dove under and swam off. He moved through the water with easy grace and reached the other bank quickly then swam back again. He got out, dripping wet. His shirt clung to the contours of muscle on his chest and stomach. The material was see-through when wet too. Quite, quite see-through.

"Hannah, are you all right? You just made a strange gurgling sound."

I coughed. "Did I?"

"Let's meet him at the door. I'm dying to know what he learned."

So was I, but I remained at the window for a few more moments, watching him cross the lawn to the house. He scanned the vicinity, as did I, but the demon didn't appear.

I didn't let out my pent-up breath until he rounded the side of the house to enter via the front door. I got up to follow Sylvia downstairs when a movement in the direction of the woods caught my eye.

A small person ran out of the dense trees so fast its legs were a blur. No, not a person.

The demon. And it was heading for Jack.

CHAPTER 9

I picked up my skirts and ran down the stairs. "Let him in! The demon is coming!"

Sylvia was ahead, but not yet at the door. I could hear footsteps drumming on the stairs behind me. Samuel.

"Open the door!" I shouted at Sylvia.

The door flew open and crashed back on its hinges before she got to it. Jack charged through and slammed it shut, just as the demon hit it from the other side. The door shook, but held, thank God.

I raced to him. He caught me in his arms, lifting me off the ground.

A violent shock drove us apart just as quickly, but at least I had that fleeting moment of feeling his arms around me, telling me without words that he was all right and he was glad to see me too. It was only a moment, but it was something and it was ours. I rubbed my arms, now damp too, but it did nothing to ease my twitching muscles or the heat swamping me.

"Did it get you?" Tommy asked, grasping Jack by the shoulders and inspecting him. I don't know when he'd arrived, but he and Samuel were both there. Bollard wheeled

Langley in too, just as the demon slammed against the door again.

Sylvia screamed.

"Stop that," Langley snapped at her. "You'll frighten the servants."

I suspected the servants would already be terrified if they'd seen that thing running out of the woods. No animal looked like a short, naked, malformed human. It was going to be hard to convince them they'd seen a wild dog.

The demon snarled and growled just beyond the door. Then it did the oddest thing. The growling stopped, and it whimpered like a child.

"In," the small voice cried. "Let in."

"Oh God," Sylvia crouched down next to her uncle's chair, her hands at her throat. "Is there someone out there with it?"

"I doubt it," Jack said, eyeing the door. Water dripped off his hair and clothes, forming a puddle on the tiles at his bare feet. He didn't seem to notice.

"Perhaps it's using the voices of the spirits it consumed to trick us," Samuel said.

Or perhaps the little ghost children wanted to get away from the demon just as much as we did. A shiver slithered down my spine, pushing the heat out of me. I hugged myself and edged closer to Sylvia and Langley.

"Why is it here?" Sylvia wailed. "What does it want?"

"Perhaps it's hungry," Jack said.

"I thought there was enough deer and other wildlife in the woods to keep it satisfied," I said.

The demon slammed against the door again. Wood splintered near the hinge.

"Get back!" Langley shouted. "Away from the door. Now!"

We did, just as the demon threw itself against the thick wood again. How much longer would the door hold up?

Sylvia began to sob. "*Do* something."

"Your fire," Tommy said to Jack.

He nodded, grim. "I can't open the door. There's a chance it'll get in before I can summon the flames." He looked at the windows on either side of the door, but dismissed those for the same reason. "I have to approach it from behind."

"That means going out again," I said. I didn't try to stop him. No one did. He had to go and there was nothing else to be done. He'd be all right. He had his fire.

But fire couldn't kill it, only scare it. My stomach churned and my heart thudded violently. Sylvia stepped up beside me and held my hand.

Jack gave us a nod then disappeared down one of the corridors that led to the service area. He would slip out that way and circle around.

Only he never got the chance.

The crack of a gunshot ripped through the air. It seemed to bounce off the hills and trees and reverberate through the house. We looked at one another, faces frozen in shock.

Jack came running back in. "Where did that come from?" he said, his gaze sweeping across all of us to reassure himself that we were unharmed.

"It sounded like a rifle," Samuel said.

"The demon's running away." Tommy pointed through the window where the creature could be seen sprinting back into the woods.

Sylvia gave a little whimper of relief.

Jack opened the door and stepped onto the porch, Tommy and Samuel at his heels. "I thought Culvert said a bullet couldn't kill it," Samuel said.

"It was probably scared off by the noise," Jack said. "As with the fire. It seems afraid of the flames."

"Whatever happened, we've got somebody to thank."

"But who?" Sylvia tried to peer past the men, but they were all too tall. "Have the Beauforts returned?"

"There!" Tommy pointed. "Coming up the driveway on horseback."

"Bloody hell," Jack muttered. "What's he doing here?"

"Who is it?" Langley asked.

"Weeks."

"The policeman?" Sylvia and I said together.

The men moved aside and we saw Weeks and a uniformed constable ride up and dismount. Weeks touched the brim of his hat and greeted us. The constable glanced nervously toward the woods. He still held a rifle, and I suspected it was loaded.

"Well," Weeks said, puffing out his narrow chest. He looked like he enjoyed being the hero of the moment. "I'd wager you're glad to see me."

"Why?" Langley said. "Did you fire the weapon or did your constable?"

Weeks deflated and removed his hat. I felt a little sorry for him. He may not have fired the weapon, but he'd at least told his man to arm himself. He deserved some thanks. "Right you are, Mr. Langley, sir. I'm only sorry he missed." He shot a glare at the constable, but the fellow was too busy watching the woods to notice.

"You aimed at it?" Samuel said. "Are you mad? You could have hit one of us through the window."

The constable flushed and stammered an apology.

"Next time, shoot into the sky," Jack said. "That'll send it running without risking lives."

"No offence, sir," Weeks said, "but we want to kill it, not let it run away. And anyways, are you sure it was a dog? Only I've never seen one that walked on two feet and had no fur."

Samuel scrubbed his hand over his face. He looked resigned and perhaps even a little sad. "Look at me, Inspector Weeks." His voice was honey-thick. "Look at my eyes and listen to my voice." Weeks' eyes became very round and he stared at Samuel. "It was a dog." Samuel clicked his fingers and Weeks blinked.

"Yes, it was a dog," the inspector echoed. "Of course it was."

Good lord! Had Samuel just hypnotized Weeks and implanted the suggestion into his head? Remarkable! He'd done it without the aid of a swaying object or any visible effort on his part. I was quite impressed, yet Samuel seemed troubled by what he'd done.

Sylvia and I exchanged glances. She suddenly looked a little uncertain about Samuel and his ability, even though it wasn't news to her. Samuel hadn't hypnotized a single member of the household since his arrival, and it was easy to forget that he had the ability. The only hypnosis I'd seen him perform was the one on me in London. No one else had been in the room with me then. Sylvia and Jack had not witnessed a hypnotism before. Whatever Jack thought of it, he kept his opinion closely guarded behind his hooded eyes.

"Might I come in?" Weeks asked. "Not sure I like standing out here with that dog wandering about." We stepped aside and the policemen entered. "You're wet," he said to Jack.

"I believe I am."

"But it's not raining."

"I know."

"Uh, the horses," I said before Weeks could question him further. "You can't leave them unguarded. What if it comes back?"

"Constable Jones here will keep watch," Weeks said.

Constable Jones swallowed heavily. I couldn't tell if he'd been hypnotized too. He gave no sign that he doubted the wild dog story. Weeks patted him on the shoulder then shoved him back out through the door.

"I'll fetch a gun and join you," Tommy offered.

"I'm not sure that's a good idea," Sylvia said. When we all looked at her, she shrugged. "Who will serve the tea?"

"Mrs. Moore," Tommy offered.

"Stay where you are, Tommy," Langley growled. "The inspector won't be staying for tea. State your business and be off, Weeks. We're very busy."

I felt quite embarrassed by his poor manners. Weeks may be an incompetent fool, but there was no need to be rude. Besides, we should be grateful that Weeks and his man had just scared off the demon. He must have something important to report, or he wouldn't have risked coming at all.

"Please step into the parlor where it's more comfortable," I said, ignoring Langley's glare. "We'd very much like to hear what you have to say."

"Uh, no thank you, Miss Smith." Weeks clutched his hat and cast an anxious glance at Langley. "I'm quite all right here. What I have to say won't take long."

"Go on then." Jack sounded gruff and impatient. With all the commotion and the visitors, I'd almost forgotten that he'd just come from the trench and dungeon. I hoped he'd found something useful that we could pass on to Mr. Culvert.

"Have you found Mr. Tate?" Sylvia asked. "His man paid us a visit last night and the sooner you can—"

"Paid you a visit?" Weeks turned to me. "I see he did not take Miss Smith."

"He tried, but I'm quite all right, thank you. A little tired today from the ordeal, but otherwise unharmed. You haven't caught him, have you?"

"No, ma'am, I regret that we haven't seen him. You didn't happen to see which direction his man ran off in?"

"Down the drive," Jack said.

Weeks's small eyes screwed up in thought until they almost disappeared in the surrounding wrinkles. "He could be anywhere."

Langley sighed and rubbed his forehead. "Then how about you send some men to look for him. You know he's in the vicinity now."

Jack shot him a warning glare and half shook his head. No doubt he thought it a bad idea to send policemen after Tate now that we suspected Ham was a demon. I tended to agree with him. As much as I wanted to have the police assisting us, it was dangerous for them, and I wouldn't be happy knowing lives were being jeopardized because of me. I was the one Tate wanted, but he seemed prepared to do anything to get me. Including ordering Ham to kill those who tried to stop him.

"We'll do our best with our limited resources, sir," Weeks said. "In the meantime, let me know immediately if he comes here again. I'd set up a watch, but you seem to have enough strong fellows to help, and what with that wild dog on the loose..." He coughed and looked away, clearly unenthusiastic about providing men.

Langley grunted. "What is it you want, Weeks?"

"I wanted to ask you, sirs, if you knew where we could find Mr. Tate's associates? One of them may know where Tate is hiding."

"We told you last time," Langley said. "We don't know anyone who knows him."

"What about his staff?"

"We only know of Ham."

"What about household staff? Sometimes people like you, sir, don't notice the servants, but a footmen or maid can hear and see a lot that goes on in a house."

"His housekeeper!" I said. "She opened the door for us that day. Has no one spoken to her, Inspector?"

He removed a notebook from his inside coat pocket and flipped the pages. "Let's see, the only member of staff interviewed by Scotland Yard was a Mrs. Dodd. Is that her?"

Langley sucked air through his teeth.

"Sir?" Weeks prompted. "Do you know her?"

Langley gave a brief shake of his head and waved the inspector's question away.

"Miss Smith?" Weeks said to me. "Was she the housekeeper?"

"I don't know," I said.

"Must be her. It says housekeeper here. Did you see no one else while you were there?"

"No," Sylvia said and I shook my head too.

"If Mrs. Dodd has already been interviewed, why the need to speak to others?" Jack asked.

"Because she was interviewed *before* Tate's escape, not after."

"Why not after?"

"They tried, but she'd moved on and they couldn't locate her."

Langley slammed his palm down on his wheelchair arm. "Incompetence is everywhere. How hard did they look?"

"August," Jack warned.

Weeks held up his hands. "Don't ask me, sir. Not my jurisdiction. I was sent a telegram to ask you about associates and staff. Seems you can't help."

"Surely they need to continue to look for the housekeeper," I said.

"It probably doesn't matter. Unlikely Tate told her where he was going to hide after breaking free from prison. I was hoping Mr. Langley here might have remembered an older associate, someone who's been with Tate since those days, or a valet perhaps. Valets are interesting. They get told things that a gentleman won't even tell his family."

"I don't know his staff," Langley ground out.

"You need to find the housekeeper," Sylvia said.

Jack nodded. "We'll look for her."

"Don't be absurd," Sylvia scoffed. "It's Scotland Yard's job to do that. Tell him, Uncle."

"I think Jack has a point. We can't rely on the police to find her."

"Now, sir, I must protest." But Weeks snapped his mouth shut upon Langley's glare.

I said nothing. I agreed with Jack. Scotland Yard might look for Mrs. Dodd, but they moved at a snail's pace. Having a demon on the loose made leaving Frakingham impossible, however. Not only that, Jack wouldn't leave me in case Ham and Tate made another attempt to kidnap me. I saw no choice but to let the police do their job.

"It's unlikely she can offer any answers," Weeks said again.

He was most likely right, but the niggling thought that she may know something remained. The name of a friend living nearby, a house once rented in Hertfordshire. And at the moment, that hope was all we had. I could see in Jack's eyes that he already felt invigorated by this new direction.

"May we have her last known address, please?" Jack said.

"I shouldn't."

"Look into my eyes, Inspector," Samuel said in his smooth, melodic voice. Weeks did as ordered, without blinking. Blankness shuttered his gaze, slackened his jaw. "Listen to me. Give Jack the address." Samuel snapped his fingers and Weeks blinked. He ripped out a page of his notebook and handed it over.

"Thank you," Jack said. Whether he was thanking Samuel or Weeks was difficult to tell. "We appreciate you coming up here to speak to us, Inspector."

Weeks put his hat on his head. "I'm only sorry you couldn't help me."

Tommy opened the front door. "Any sign of the dog?" Jack called to Constable Jones, standing by the horses.

"No, sir."

The policemen mounted and rode off. Once they were out of sight, we returned inside.

"Surely Mrs. Dodd won't know where to find Tate," Sylvia said. "She was only his housekeeper after all."

Jack shot a glance at Bollard of all people. "You'd be surprised at how much some staff know."

"That you would," Tommy muttered.

"That will be all, Tommy," Langley snapped.

Tommy sighed and trudged off. Sylvia watched him go, her cheeks pink and steam practically rising from her ears. Langley, in turn, watched her.

"He forgets his place sometimes," she said to nobody in particular.

"Leave him be, Syl," said Jack.

I moved to the window, but the policemen had already disappeared around the bend in the drive. "Even if Mrs. Dodd can't tell us where to find Tate, perhaps she can tell us more about him. His habits, his state of mind, anything that might give us a clue to his whereabouts."

"It's a slim chance, but we have to take it," Jack said. "There are no other options. I'll leave today."

"Take Hannah with you," said Langley.

"I intend to."

Sylvia held up her hands for silence. "Have you both gone mad? Hannah can't go. It's much too dangerous for her out there with Tate on the loose. And what about the other demon? With Jack gone, who will protect us?"

"Hannah's safest with me, and I'm going to London to find Mrs. Dodd. Besides, Frakingham isn't much of a haven for her right now. If she leaves without Tate knowing, we have the upper hand."

"That doesn't help those of us who must face his wrath once he realizes he's been tricked."

"Tommy will be here, and Samuel and Olsen. Everyone will be armed. We saw the effect gunfire had on the demon, perhaps it will work on Ham too."

"I doubt it," she muttered. "It didn't run away from the fire in Tate's factory. If it wasn't afraid of fire like the other demon, it may not be afraid of bullets either."

She had a point. One that got us all thinking until Samuel spoke. "I'll come to London too."

Jack shook his head. "You're needed here."

"I agree," Langley put in.

"Hear me out," Samuel said. "If Mrs. Dodd proves loyal to Tate and won't answer questions, I can hypnotize her."

Langley grunted. "You have to find her first."

"It's worth a try," Sylvia said.

I watched Samuel, trying to gauge if he did indeed *want* to hypnotize anyone. He'd seemed quite upset at having to do it to Weeks. It was difficult to tell, however. I suspected he was as much a master of hiding his true emotions as he was of charming people.

"That leaves only Tommy here." Jack shook his haed. "I'm not sure I like those odds."

"There'll also be Olsen and Bollard," Samuel said. "And Langley. They're all capable of firing a weapon or using fire."

But what if those things weren't enough? I didn't want to voice my concerns. For one thing, Sylvia was terrified enough. She was already repeating her protest for a second time.

"We won't be gone long," Samuel told her. "A few days at most."

"You must return in three days," Langley said. "Even if you don't find her. Understand, Jack?"

"We'll find her," Jack said. "I don't want to stay away longer than necessary anyway. It's too dangerous."

Langley nodded, apparently satisfied. He signaled to his man to wheel him away.

"I also want to see Culvert while we're there," Jack said.

"That reminds me," I said. "Did you discover anything in the trench?"

"As a matter of fact, yes."

Langley paused near the arched doorway and Bollard turned him around to face us. "What did you find?"

Jack pulled a medallion out of his pocket and handed it to his uncle. "It was half buried in the dirt near the dungeon entrance."

Langley turned it over in his palm and ran the pad of his thumb around the edge. It was flat and round with a star carved in the middle. "It's made of bronze and the workmanship is crude. It looks old."

Sylvia stood over him and peered down at the medallion. "There's a small hole at the edge. Perhaps it was attached to a chain or strap. It may have been worn as a necklace. Any idea how old it is?"

Nobody did. "We can have an expert look at it in London," Samuel suggested.

"I want to take it to Culvert first," Jack said. "I think it was used to bring the demon here."

I accepted the flat disc and studied it. "He did mention amulets and incantations. Is that another term for curse?"

"I believe so, in this context."

"I wonder how the demon got into the dungeon."

"I don't know." Jack nodded at the amulet. "But this proves that someone deliberately summoned it."

Sylvia gasped. "Good lord. Who would do such a thing? Tate? Why when he already has Ham?"

It was a very good question. None of us had an answer.

CHAPTER 10

Jack and Samuel rode on the driver's seat, leaving me inside the carriage on my own. I slept some of the way, read for a while, or simply stared out the window at the passing scenery—after we'd left Frakingham well behind, that is. They'd wanted me to keep the curtains closed until we were on the main London road in case Tate and Ham were watching.

We stayed overnight at an inn and arrived the next morning at the last known address of Mrs. Dodd. It was a large, white house in the exclusive suburb of Kensington. I was surprised that she had been living in such a magnificent place, until I realized that she would have lived in the servants' area. It wasn't her house, but that of her new employers. I wondered why she hadn't stayed in service there very long since it was quite the step up from keeping house for a mad scientist.

We soon found out that she hadn't been employed there at all.

"Her sister is," said the maid who answered our knock at the service entrance. The Kensington house was built in an older style with the servants' area in the basement below street level. It had its own set of stairs beside the main ones. We'd decided to speak to the servants and not go through the family at all. It proved a good idea. The maid was quite talkative. "Mrs. Perry is the housekeeper here," she said. "When that Mrs. Dodd turned up two weeks back, Mrs. Perry took her in. Much to the butler's disgust, mind. It's against the rules to have people to stay, see. But Mrs. Dodd, she says she's desperate, and it'll only be for a few days until she can find her feet."

"When did she leave?" I asked.

"Just a few days after she arrived, true to her word."

"Do you know where she went?" Jack asked.

"No."

I looked to Samuel. He gave a slight shake of his head. He wouldn't hypnotize her. Like me, he must think the maid knew nothing of Mrs. Dodd's current whereabouts. Or perhaps he simply didn't want to do it.

"May we speak to Mrs. Perry?" I asked.

"I'll fetch her." She went to walk off, but thought better of it. "Who are you then? You ain't police," she said with a jerk of her chin at me. Women weren't allowed on the police force.

"We're private enquiry agents," I said. "Our client would like to find Mrs. Dodd to settle a…private matter."

That seemed to satisfy her and she headed off down the corridor, leaving us standing in the doorway. "Private enquiry agent?" Jack said, a smile twitching his lips.

"It seemed like an interesting occupation. I've always wanted to be one ever since reading Poe's *Murders in the Rue Morgue*."

Jack and Samuel both laughed. "I don't know why you brought me along," Samuel said. "You seem to be able to get people to talk on your own, Hannah."

"Shhh," I whispered. "Here she comes."

Mrs. Perry was a short, stocky woman who puffed as she walked. The great bunch of keys dangling from her waist jangled with each rolling step. I wondered how she coped working in such a large house, but then again most of the laborious tasks would have been done by the maids.

"Why are you asking after my sister?" she said before she reached us. A deep line cut her forehead in half as if continuous frowning had worn a permanent groove there. She had a mouth set like a bulldog, turned down at the corners and disappearing into the folds of her chin.

"She's all yours, Gladstone," Jack muttered.

"Grouchy old matrons are my specialty," Samuel said without moving his lips. He bowed to the housekeeper and when he straightened, he had one of his most charming smiles in place.

"What're you smiling at me like that for?" Mrs. Perry snapped. "I haven't got time for boys like you who think they can pull the wool over the eyes of the likes of me. State your business and move on."

I tried not to laugh, but a snigger escaped despite my best efforts.

"Something amusing, Miss?"

I gulped and my laughter caught in my throat, choking me. I spluttered and coughed, and my eyes watered. Mrs. Perry clicked her tongue and turned back to Samuel. She forked her brows and said, "Well?"

"I, uh…" He cleared his throat.

"We want to speak to your sister," Jack said, taking over after all.

"She's not here." Mrs. Perry went to close the door.

Jack stepped over the threshold and pressed his hand to the door. "Do you know where we can find her?"

All four of her chins shook with indignation. "Does this have something to do with that man she kept house for?"

"Yes."

"He's in jail, and she's well rid of him. Whatever he did, it's nothing to do with her. That's what I told the police. Good day."

Jack did not let go of the door. "We still need to speak to her. Tate has escaped and—"

"Escaped!" She rubbed her hand over her mouth and blinked at Jack. "Why didn't the police tell me?"

"They didn't think it necessary."

"Fools," she spat. "Her life may be in danger."

"Why? Does she know something important?"

"I doubt it, but the fellow was mad. Who knows what he's capable of."

"We need to speak to her," I said. "We need to know where Tate is now."

"Why?"

"He wants to kidnap Miss Smith." Jack nodded at me. "We need to stop him before he gets to her."

She looked at each of us in turn, rubbing her jaw some more. "I don't see how talking to my sister can help you. Having you or the police poking about will draw attention and endanger her life. I can't have that."

Jack leaned closer, using his superior height to intimidate. She did not shrink away. She looked like the sturdy sort who would meet an oncoming train with a scowl and crossed arms. "Mrs. Perry, listen to me," he said. "This is important."

"Jack." Samuel placed a hand on Jack's shoulder. "Let me speak to her." The change in his voice and demeanor was remarkable. It was as if he'd turned on the charm like water from a tap. There was an odd look in his eyes too. The blueness had softened and somehow deepened. I felt like I could fall into them, and he wasn't even looking at me.

Jack poked my shoulder to get my attention. There was no spark, and I felt no surge of heat—it wasn't a sensual touch, but a warning. He indicated I should step behind Samuel and I did. I instantly felt more in control of myself and not quite so dazed, although tiredness still pulled at me. Indeed, I'd not been able to shake the tiredness all week.

Jack's glare was unrelenting and off-putting. He didn't seem at all affected by Samuel's hypnotic voice. I looked away and listened to Samuel as he spoke to Mrs. Perry. Now that I wasn't gazing into his eyes, I could appreciate the deep, rich cadence of his voice. It washed over me like warm milk, made me want to capture it somehow and hold it.

Jack poked me again. *Stop listening,* he mouthed.

I can't, I mouthed back. The pull of Samuel's voice was remarkably strong. Fortunately it changed as he asked his first question.

"Tell me where Mrs. Dodd is."

"She got a new position," intoned Mrs. Perry. Her eyes were huge as she stared back at Samuel. "Housekeeper for a Mr. and Mrs. Gearsley."

"The address?"

"Number twenty Patterson Street, Hampstead."

"Thank you, Mrs. Perry. Now, when you wake—"

"Come inside, dear sir." Mrs. Perry took Samuel's hand and pulled him toward her. She used such force that he lost his balance and ended up in her arms. He tried to extricate himself, but Mrs. Perry had quite the hold around his waist. "Let me fetch you some cake and tea."

"Uh, thank you, but no."

"Come now, dear boy." She rubbed his back. Samuel wrenched himself free. He took a step away, almost knocking me over.

"When you wake you'll remember nothing," he said quickly. He clicked his fingers. "Wake up!"

Mrs. Perry blinked slowly. For a fleeting moment she appeared quite dazed, then her eyes focused on Samuel. Her bulldog jowls wobbled. "Are you still here? Be off with you."

"Yes, of course." Samuel bowed. "Thank you, Mrs. Perry."

She grunted and shut the door.

Samuel fidgeted with his tie and blew out a measured breath. "Let's go."

I kept my laughter in until we'd rounded the corner and I could control it no longer. "Does that always happen?" I said between giggles.

Samuel's face had gone red to the roots of his fair hair. "Not every single time."

"But a lot?"

He nodded and avoided my gaze. He was walking very fast, but Jack was walking faster up ahead. I had to trot to keep up with them both. "That was highly amusing," I said. "I wonder what would have happened if you'd not ended the session."

"I'm glad I provided some amusement in these dark days," Samuel said. He appeared to be fighting a smile, but when he glanced sideways at me, he lost the battle. "I'm going to have nightmares for a week now."

"So if you can do that without a swaying object, why did you use that disc on me in Dr. Werner's rooms?"

"It's just a prop. People expect me to use one, Dr. Werner included. It makes them feel more comfortable when I conform to their image of what a hypnotist should do."

Jack stopped and swung round. He wasn't laughing. Indeed, he looked furious.

"Jack?" I asked. "What's wrong?"

He pointed back the way we'd come. "That! I can't believe—" He shook his head, spun on his heel, and strode off again, faster than before.

"Jack!"

He didn't stop.

"Jack, slow down, I can't keep up."

He stopped, but kept his back to us. He was breathing hard. His entire body seemed to expand with every inhalation. I wanted to massage the rigidity out of his shoulders, but there would be no touching of that nature between us, even if it were acceptable in public.

"What is it?" I asked, standing as close as I dared. "What's wrong?"

He gave one shake of his head, but said nothing.

"I thought that's what you wanted me to do," Samuel said. He sounded a little hurt at Jack's anger, and I could understand why. We *had* wanted him to hypnotize Mrs. Perry.

Jack turned around and pinned Samuel with a pointed

glare. "I can't believe I let you hypnotize Hannah before!"

"Ah," was all Samuel said.

"That's it?" Jack fisted his hands at his sides, but not before I saw the reddened tips from the fire boiling inside him. "That's all you have to say on the matter?"

One eye on Jack's fists, Samuel said, "You're not going to hit me or throw a fireball, are you?"

Jack growled and walked off. Once again I had to run to keep up. "You didn't *let* Samuel hypnotize me," I said. "Indeed, you didn't have a choice."

"I remember," he bit off. "I also remember you throwing me out of the room. I shouldn't have let you do that either."

"Jack, I was perfectly all right. Dr. Werner was there too, and you know Samuel now. He's an honorable man."

"Thank you, Hannah," Samuel said. "If I wasn't honorable, I would have taken Mrs. Perry up on her offer."

"Samuel!" I cried. "That's not helping."

"Of *cake*," he said, grinning. Good lord, he was making it worse. Jack looked like he wanted to rip Samuel's head off. "Go on, Langley, hit me. I know you want to, and it'll make you feel better."

Jack stopped.

"Jack!" I scolded. "Don't you dare."

He grunted and continued walking toward our carriage. He flipped a coin to each of the two lads holding the reins and opened the door for me as Samuel climbed onto the driver's seat.

"Although I find your concern flattering," I said to Jack, "you are not to take out your frustration on Samuel. Understand? We went to him, and he did nothing wrong."

He fingered the lace cuff of my jacket. Heat bloomed at my wrist and spread up my arm, but not to an uncomfortable level. "It's just that…" He sighed again. "For the first time, I saw his power work on a female. Mrs. Perry's reaction was startling. If that's how most of the women are when he hypnotizes them…"

"I assure you I didn't swoon or offer Samuel…cake. I

was quite blank thanks to the memory blockage put on me as a child." Some of the anger left his eyes, so I didn't feel quite so bad at telling the small lie. Of course I had no way of knowing how I'd behaved in my hypnotized state. If I'd behaved as Mrs. Perry had, neither Samuel nor Dr. Werner had said so. Of course, they wouldn't. If that sort of thing became public, Dr. Werner would be put out of business from the ensuing scandal.

"Come on," I said, "ride with me in the cabin. Samuel can find his way to number twenty Patterson Street, Hampstead on his own."

Finally Jack's anger dissolved completely with the cracking of a smile. "How can I refuse an invitation like that?"

***

The Hampstead house where Mrs. Dodd worked was nothing like the Kensington house. It was modern and built over two levels with no basement service area accessible from the street. We knocked on the front door and, as we'd hoped, Mrs. Dodd opened it.

She recognized Jack and I, but I could see her struggling to remember where from. But the moment came and when it did, she gasped. "Good lord, you were at Mr. Tate's on that awful day."

"Good afternoon, Mrs. Dodd," Jack said. "I'm Jack Langley and this is Miss Hannah Smith and Mr. Samuel Gladstone. We've come to talk to you about Reuben Tate. May we come in?"

She glanced over her shoulder, and came out to us on the porch. She closed the door behind her. "My new employers are strict about me having visitors," she said with a tired sigh. "And I don't want them aware of my connection to a man like Tate. I still cannot believe he turned into such a monster."

I was relieved that Mrs. Dodd wasn't at all like her sister. She didn't shut the door in our face when we mentioned Tate for a start.

"How did you find me?" she asked. "Did my sister tell you where I worked?"

"Mrs. Perry was a little reluctant at first," Jack said.

"She's very protective of me. I'm her little sister, you see, and after what happened that day with Mr. Tate...well, she worries. I hope she wasn't too curt with you. How did you convince her to give you this address?"

"Mr. Gladstone can be very persuasive."

Samuel bowed and smiled that lovely smile of his.

"He must be," Mrs. Dodd said, eyeing him with open curiosity. "My sister is not the easily persuaded sort."

"Mrs. Dodd, we need to speak to you about Mr. Tate," I said. "We have some important questions in light of his escape."

"Escape!" She gasped. "I had no idea. Dear God, what is our prison system coming to if it allows a man like him to get out?"

"I think the circumstances took even his jailors by surprise," Jack said. "We need to talk to you about him. You may be able to help us find him before he finds us. He's after Miss Smith, you see, for reasons too numerous to go into now."

Another gasp. "You poor dear. Of course I'll try to help, but I doubt I'll know anything useful."

"How long have you worked for him?"

"Oh, years." She counted on her fingers. "At least twenty."

Twenty! Then she'd been with Tate when Langley partnered him. Odd how he'd not mentioned it.

Jack obviously had the same thought, because he said, "I think you may know more than you realize. Is there somewhere we can go to talk?"

"Not here, not now. What about later this afternoon? I can meet you after I've served Mrs. Gearsley's tea. Cook can make the dinner preparations without me, as long as I'm back to serve."

"Is there an inn nearby?"

"The Hammer and Nail is a block away." She pointed down the street. "Turn right then left. Meet me at four-thirty."

We thanked her and she slipped back inside the house, giving us an uncertain smile before closing the final gap.

"We have several hours before we meet her," Samuel said as we walked back to the carriage. "What shall we do now?"

"Speak to Culvert," Jack said. "I want to show him the amulet."

***

We ate lunch at a coffee house not far from George Culvert's residence then drove on to his house. He lived in an elegantly curved street of Belgravia where magnificent residences reigned over the vista. He wasn't at home, but his lovely wife Adelaide—Jacob Beaufort's sister—told us we would find him at the charity school for orphans. Apparently he taught there sometimes, although what a demonologist taught to a group of children was a mystery.

The school was located on the edge of Clerkenwell, an area patterned with narrow alleys crammed with small workshops and equally small houses. Signs in the doors and windows informed passersby what sort of trade was conducted inside. That's if you could see the signs in the first place. Between the grimy window glass and the lack of sunlight reaching the deep recesses of the alleys, most were obscured. Children played in the street, and I was glad to see they all wore shoes and coats to ward off the bitter cold. Not that I felt it, but Samuel did. He blew on his gloved hands and hunched into his coat. I was glad for my internal fire for once.

Jack paid two older lads to mind the horses and coach while we went into the school. The building was the largest on the street, its windows the cleanest. We were met by a maid who showed us through to a small, comfortable parlor, then left us to fetch Mr. Culvert.

It wasn't him who entered a few minutes later, however, but a tall striking blonde woman. Going by Jack's soft exhalation of breath, I guessed she was Charity, the teacher. His lover.

I was quite pleased with how I maintained a serene composure. My polite smile didn't slip and my hands remained loosely clasped in my lap, not a white knuckle on show. I didn't once glance at Jack. I couldn't have borne any wistful or longing looks he may have cast in her direction. To anyone who'd looked at me, I would have appeared calm and composed.

Yet my insides were a bundle of tangled knots in danger of unraveling at any moment. It would have been easier if Miss Charity weren't so pretty or so elegant. She had a perfectly oval face with not a freckle in sight, and the loveliest fair hair. Being tall meant she could carry off the plain black dress with the neat bustle at the back with elegance. The dress's only adornments were the large cuffs that covered part of her hands. She made me feel quite overdone in the ruches and swathes of my dark green silk gown.

"Jack," she cooed. "I cannot believe it's you."

"Charity," he said and bowed.

She laughed a throaty laugh and bid him not to be so formal with her. "When was it we last saw one another?"

"A year ago. You left the children all of a sudden without word." There was no accusation in his tone. It was merely a statement of fact.

Her smile vanished and a shadow passed over her face. "Ah yes. That." She did not explain or apologize, but turned her smile back on again. It seemed she and I both knew how to do the correct and polite thing in certain company. "Won't you introduce me to your friends?"

Jack cleared his throat. I still refused to look at his face, but it was getting more and more difficult. "This is Miss Hannah Smith, my cousin's companion, and this is Mr. Samuel Gladstone, a neurologist undertaking research at Frakingham."

She bobbed a small curtsey. "What an interesting

combination of people you have at that house, Jack. Are you studying anyone in particular for your research, Mr. Gladstone?"

"I'm a student of all human nature, Miss…"

"Charity. I'm Miss Charity to everyone from the students to the other teachers."

"Miss Charity." Samuel smiled and I was quite certain his was genuine. It would seem the beauty of Miss Charity could charm the charmer himself. "As I said, I'm a student of human nature. I observe how people think and behave in all sorts of situations. I study everyone I meet. The inhabitants of Frakingham House are no exception."

"I'm sure they give you much material for your research. Particularly Jack here," she said, her eyes twinkling with merry mischief.

"Oh? How so?"

"Charity," Jack said, his voice a low warning. It was such a change that I broke my rule and looked at him. He was glaring at Charity, but she was ignoring him.

"That's up to you to find out, Mr. Gladstone." She leaned closer, conspiratorial, but Jack and I could hear every word. "Dig beneath the surface of that steely façade he so expertly wears. Ask questions of the *right* people, and you'll find out more about Jack *Cutler* than you ever wanted to know." The use of his original name wasn't lost on anyone. Samuel's gaze slid to Jack then me, then back to Charity. "Indeed," she went on, "you may wish you'd never asked."

She finally looked at Jack then, but I was surprised by what I saw in her eyes. I expected triumph that her cutting remarks had brought such a reaction, perhaps even a measure of desperation since I was quite sure she was trying to gain his attention. But there was none of that in her demeanor. Only sadness that seemed to run like a stain through her pretty blue eyes. And something else too. Something that took my breath away and tightened my chest.

Fear.

Charity was afraid of Jack.

What had happened between the two of them all those years ago? I wanted to know, but tension wrapped its tentacles around us, and I felt compelled to break its hold.

"It's very nice to meet you, Miss Charity," I said.

"I'm sorry, Miss Smith, I've been terribly impolite." She did seem genuinely apologetic. "You're a friend to Jack's cousin? How delightful. I've met Miss Langley and she seems like a sweet girl."

"She's been very kind to me."

"She's not here with you?" Naturally she must be curious as to why Sylvia's companion was gallivanting around London with two gentlemen and not Sylvia herself. It must seem terribly suspicious.

"Circumstances have necessitated she remain at Frakingham and Hannah come with me," Jack said.

Miss Charity raised an eyebrow. Clearly she didn't miss the use of 'me' instead of 'us.' "How delightful."

"Not really. A madman has escaped prison and is trying to kidnap her."

Her eyes widened and her jaw dropped. "My God. That's truly awful." For the first time I felt she'd said something that didn't have a double meaning and wasn't designed to tease or cajole Jack. "Does it have anything to do with you needing to see Mr. Culvert?"

"Yes. Is he here?"

"He's teaching at the moment, but his class should be almost finished. The maid has been given instructions to tell him you're waiting for him. Can I get you any refreshments?"

"No, thank you," I said.

She sat with us, which I found a little awkward. She had not looked at Jack again, but he couldn't keep his eyes off her. He studied her intently, his gaze taking in every part of her until finally resting on her hands. She'd folded them in her lap. The extravagant cuffs reached almost to her knuckles.

"Tell me about yourself, Miss Smith," she said. "Why is the escapee after you?"

"Well," I said on a breath as I considered whether I wanted to tell her anything and if so, how much.

"It's complicated," Jack said before I could go on.

Charity sat back as if his words had pushed her. "Of course. I'm sorry. I shouldn't have asked." She rose. "Let me see if Mr. Culvert is finished."

I waited until she'd left before I turned to Jack. Samuel got in first, however. "Was it necessary to be so short with her, Langley? It was a natural question. Of course she'd be curious."

"There are some things Charity shouldn't know." His gaze settled on me. "You understand, don't you, Hannah?"

I didn't, not really, but I told him I did. He seemed to want me to agree with him, understand him. I couldn't imagine why. Ever since seeing Charity, Jack hadn't been his usual confident self. Not that he seemed afraid or desperate, but there was something lacking in his composure.

And then it struck me. He cared about her opinion of him. I suddenly realized that not telling her why Tate was after me had been difficult for Jack, and that's perhaps why it had come out sounding so curt. I think he'd wanted to tell her everything. So why hadn't he?

Whatever the reason, it would seem Jack hadn't quite gotten over his feelings for her after all.

A large hammer smashed through my rib cage—or that's how it felt. I wanted to run out of the parlor and let the tears welling in my eyes flow. But Jack was watching me closely and I felt like he could see right through the smashed ribs to my fragile heart.

"Hannah," he said softly.

I was saved from my self-pity by the entrance of George Culvert. Charity wasn't with him. I found I was quite happy about that.

"Has something happened?" he asked even before greeting us. "Has it harmed anyone?"

"No," Jack said, "nothing like that."

Mr. Culvert pushed his glasses up his nose and let out a

deep breath. "That is a relief. In that case, you must have more information for me."

"We do. We found this." Jack pulled the amulet out of his pocket.

Mr. Culvert shut the parlor door then took the amulet and inspected it. "Was it in the trench?"

"Yes, half buried in the soil on the trench floor."

"Ah." He picked at the central star shape with his fingernail and muttered some "hmmm" and "ah-ha" noises. "I'd say this is probably what was used to summon it."

"Probably?" Samuel asked. "Can't you be more definite than that?"

"I'm afraid not, Mr. Gladstone. It's impossible to tell for certain, but if it was found near the dungeon, then it's likely to be the amulet that was used. It does have a likeness to others I've seen."

"I'm not sure I like the uncertainty in your answer."

Mr. Culvert merely shrugged and handed the amulet back to Jack. "I sent an incantation via the mail, but it wouldn't have reached you before you left. Dine with my wife and I tonight, and I'll write it out again for you."

"Thank you," Jack said.

"Capital! I've been telling my wife what an interesting time we had at Frakingham and she's regretted not coming ever since."

"Before we go," I said, "is there somewhere I can freshen up?"

"Of course." He opened the door and gave me directions.

I went in search of Miss Charity instead. I couldn't pass up the opportunity to speak to her alone and find out more about Jack—and about her relationship with him. I wasn't sure if I'd find out anything good. Indeed, I was quite sure I wouldn't, but I *had* to know.

CHAPTER 11

I found Miss Charity in a classroom speaking to two girls of about ten years of age. She was pointing at something in the book one of them held open.

"Excuse me, Miss Charity," I said. "May I have a word?"

She dismissed the girls. As they passed me, both brushed their fingers along my skirt. One of them sighed, the other blinked large eyes up at me then ran off when I said hello.

"Forgive them," Miss Charity said, smiling. "They're rather in awe of you."

"Me! Whatever for?"

She indicated my dark green day dress and jacket, my matching hat with the flowers around the brim. "You look so elegant to them. Rather like Mrs. Beaufort. She always elicits a few gawps from the girls."

"You flatter me by comparing me to her, Miss Charity."

She merely shrugged. "What can I do for you, Miss Smith? I assume you've sought me out for a reason. Does Jack know you're here?"

"The gentlemen think I'm freshening up."

"Ah." She indicated I should sit in one of the chairs angled near her desk. I did and she sat behind the desk. "You want to know more about Jack." It wasn't a question.

"Is it that obvious?"

"No, but I'm a woman too and Jack is..." She sighed. "Jack is compelling."

I clasped my hands tighter in my lap. "Do *you* find him compelling, Miss Charity?"

She hesitated. "Not as much as I used to."

"Why?"

She seemed shocked by my bluntness and took another moment to answer. "I suppose because I know most of his secrets now. The ones he knows the answers to himself, that is."

"And what are those secrets?"

She gave a short laugh. "Miss Smith, you can't possibly expect me to answer that. If Jack wants you to know, then he'll tell you."

"How can he answer me when I don't know which questions to ask?"

She lifted one shoulder. "A fair point. Let me tell you this then. I can see that Jack likes you very much. It's written all over his face."

It was? In that case, I must be illiterate because I couldn't see it when Miss Charity was in the room.

"It's because of that, and because you've been direct with me, that I'm going to be direct with you. Jack and I were very close once. We remained friends even after he moved to Frakingham. We don't dislike each other, Miss Smith. I can assure you, however, that he and I are not as...close as we once were. Our friendship has waned with the passing of time. We're both happier that way." She tugged on her sleeves, but not before I saw a scar on the back of one of her hands. A broad scar that covered almost the entire hand.

A burn scar.

I sucked in air and tried to think of something to say. "It's just that you two acted so oddly in the parlor just now."

She looked down at her hands and pulled on the cuffs again even though the scar was no longer visible. "Jack and I

PLAYING WITH FIRE

have a long, turbulent history together. We've hurt each other too many times to count."

Bile rose to my throat. No. He wouldn't. But I had to ask. "How did he hurt you?"

"Not like that," she said quickly. "Never physically. The sort of pain we inflicted on each other doesn't leave scars. It was never intentional. He's a good man is Jack Langley."

"Jack Cutler, you mean."

She gave me a tired smile. "Yes. Jack Cutler, man of fire and master thief by the age of eight."

"A thief?" I muttered. Perhaps it should have been obvious to me considering his upbringing, but it wasn't.

"Don't tell him I told you." The mischievous twinkle returned to her eyes. "It's how we all survived. We'd have nothing to eat in those days if we didn't steal. Jack could keep us warm with the point of a finger, but he could also keep us fed with those same fingers. He was incredibly fast at picking pockets. Most victims were never aware of what had happened until he was well away, and those that did detect him in the process could never catch him. He was fast on his feet too."

"Yes, I've seen him."

"I imagine you have." She folded her hands and I thought our conversation was over, that she'd told me as much as she wanted to, but then she spoke again. "Jack saved me, you know. He saved me many times."

"From what?"

"From all sorts of things, and people, but mostly from myself." Tears shone in her eyes, but didn't spill. "I'll be forever grateful to him for that, and he'll always hold a special place in my heart. But it's time to move on. I *want* to move on, and I want him to as well. I'm glad I met you, Miss Smith. It makes me hopeful for his future."

I found Miss Charity utterly confounding. I'd gone from thinking she still loved Jack to the complete opposite and then to somewhere in the middle. I suppose relationships of their nature were complicated, but I'd never had experience of them. My long-term relationships were with only two people, Miss Levine and Vi. Neither would be receiving social calls from me now.

"You'd better go," Charity said. "They'll be wondering where you got to."

"Yes. Of course." I stood. "Just one more thing. There's something I need to ask you and you probably won't answer me, but I'll regret it if I don't."

"This sounds intriguing."

"I think something happened to Jack. Something to do with his fire that makes him reluctant to use it on people, even if it's to save somebody. Do you know why?"

She bit her lower lip then released it to smile, albeit thinly. She took my arm and walked slowly with me to the door. "You ask too many questions, Miss Smith, and that's one that he must tell you himself. If he wants to."

"I thought as much."

"But you had to try," she quipped. "I understand." We stopped at the door and she turned to face me. "Be assured, Miss Smith, if he does tell you, it means he cares for you very deeply. It's not something he would want just anyone to know."

"Thank you. I'm glad we spoke."

"As am I. Take care. I hope you catch that madman. I suspect there's a story there, and I love a good story. You'll have to return one day and tell it to me. I'm sure we'll meet again now that I'm working here. I know Jack will want to see the Plum Alley children from time to time. He always felt responsible for them, even those who came after he'd left."

I took her hands, but she pulled away and tugged the cuffs again. She'd said Jack hadn't hurt her, but had he caused those scars somehow?

Oh lord. It suddenly struck me why he'd not told her about Tate and me. I'd thought it was because he didn't want to explain the whole mess, but perhaps it was because Charity had been burned. Was she afraid of fire? Was that why she looked at Jack with fear earlier? Was that why he hadn't told her about my fire, because he didn't want her to be afraid of *me*?

It explained her mixed emotions toward him too.

I opened my mouth to ask, but shut it again. Sometimes not asking questions was the wisest move, and I suspected this was one of those times.

I bid her good day and thanked her again. I made my way back to the parlor where the three men were discussing all things demonic. Mr. Culvert walked us out to the carriage where a cluster of children had gathered around the horses. Jack paid the lads who'd minded it and suggested to Samuel that he drive again. Samuel claimed not to mind. He winked at me, and I realized he suspected Jack was purposely keeping him away from me. I wondered if it were true. Surely Jack knew Samuel wouldn't hypnotize me against my will.

We had tea at the Hammer and Nail while we waited for Mrs. Dodd. It was a crooked old inn with low ceiling beams and an enormous yawning hearth. A few drinkers who appeared as ancient as the inn sat hunched over their ales at the bar. They didn't move except to lift their glasses to their mouths. We sat in the corner and kept our voices low as we discussed the demon.

"I'm so glad we have the amulet and will soon have an appropriate incantation with which to send it back," I said.

Jack agreed. "Now if we only knew for certain whether Tate summoned it to Frakingham."

"If it wasn't him, then who?" I asked. "And why?"

Both Jack and Samuel shrugged. "Culvert suggested the summoning isn't always accurate," Samuel said. "Perhaps it ended up in the dungeon by accident and was meant for somewhere else. Somewhere far from Frakingham."

"If you believe that, then you're a fool," Jack told him.

"I've been called worse."

"I'm sure you have."

"Do you have a problem with me, *Cutler*?"

I held my breath and glanced at Jack's face and then his

hands, but he didn't look angry, and there were no sparks. I breathed again.

"You have questions," Jack said.

"Several." Samuel smiled, but it wasn't one of his hypnotic ones. He wasn't trying to charm Jack, although he may have been trying to placate him. Samuel couldn't afford to make an enemy of him. "Tell me about Miss Charity. How did you two meet?"

Jack lifted an eyebrow. "So the mesmerist got mesmerized."

"I'm not a mesmerist. I'm simply curious about you two."

Jack grunted. "We were orphans together, living on the streets."

Samuel sat back in his chair and didn't take his eyes off Jack. "Go on. Tell me everything."

Jack did indeed tell Samuel everything. At least, everything that I already knew. He left out nothing, not even the part where he and Charity had been lovers, although he didn't express it in quite so bald terms.

Samuel was silent for a long time afterward. He made no comments, and it was impossible to tell from his face what he thought of it all. I was just wondering how to break the unsettling silence when Jack spoke again.

"I've answered your questions, now you answer mine," he said." Why are you at Frakingham?"

Samuel crossed his arms and for a moment I thought he'd refuse to answer. But he must have thought better of it because he let out a long breath and nodded. "I came to study Hannah."

"Me!"

"After hypnotizing you in Dr. Werner's rooms, I decided I'd had enough of trying to cure hysteria and melancholy in ladies with nothing better to do than think up ailments for themselves. I needed to work with people with real problems related to hypnosis, and you were the only one I knew about. I hoped to find out more about the memory block that was put on you, and study how it affected your thought patterns and behavior."

"But the block has been lifted. You know that."

"August Langley suggested that I remain at Frakingham anyway. I felt comfortable there, being something of a freak myself, so I took him up on the offer."

Jack held up his hand. "Wait. You're telling us you're not doing anything at all at Frakingham? No research, no studies? You're wasting our time and money, Gladstone."

"*You* don't do anything there," Samuel shot back.

"I manage the estate and August's financial interests. He wants to work purely on his science these days."

Samuel accepted this was a nod. "I can assure you, I am not wasting anything. I'm conducting research into my hypnosis as well as observing the behavior and thought patterns on everyone in the house."

"Whatever for?" I asked. "I mean, I understand you wish to know more about your ability, and that's only natural, but *our* behavior? Why?"

"You're a small community with little outside influence. Two of you have extraordinary paranormal abilities, another is a mute, one is a temperamental cripple, and Sylvia is…well, she's just Sylvia. Having a normal member in the household is helpful as a control."

"I don't know if my cousin could be described as normal," Jack muttered.

"Each of you behaves in a certain way under certain circumstances, and that in turn affects your thinking and actions. That's how the neurological aspect enters the equation. I'm merely observing at the moment and then I'll try to make conclusions. I may even devise some specific tests."

"I'm not sure I like being part of an experiment," I said.

"I know I certainly don't," Jack said, glaring at Samuel. "You'll not wire me up to any machines."

Samuel smiled. "Don't worry. It won't hurt."

Jack's eyes narrowed further.

"Here's Mrs. Dodd," I said, looking past Jack's shoulder.

"Behave nicely, or she won't give us any answers."

"Yes she will, because Samuel'll make her."

"I won't hypnotize unless I have to," Samuel whispered as Mrs. Dodd walked up.

We greeted her and she sat beside me. Jack ordered her a glass of sherry and another for me. He and Samuel drank ale.

"Twenty years is a long time to work for someone," I said as way of beginning the conversation.

"Actually it was more," she said. "I started just after my husband died. He was a foreman in one of the factories in Hackney Wick and there was an accident."

"How awful. I'm terribly sorry, Mrs. Dodd."

She thanked me and sipped her sherry. She was a gentle-looking woman with warm eyes and soft features. I could see the resemblance with her sister in her loose cheeks and chins, her large bosom, but it ended there. Fortunately she seemed more eager than her sister to talk.

"Do you know where Tate might be hiding now?" Jack asked. "Does he have a house in Hertfordshire or friends there?"

She shook her head. "He doesn't have friends."

"None?" Samuel asked. "That's odd. What about female companions?"

Mrs. Dodd sipped her sherry and kept on sipping.

"Mrs. Dodd?" I prompted.

She set the glass down. "I, uh... Well. I've never known him to have a *female* companion."

Perhaps she didn't understand. "Mr. Gladstone is referring to company," I said. "Of the, er, intimate nature."

"I know."

"So..."

"Hannah," Jack whispered. He shook his head, warning me. I got the distinct feeling I'd missed something. Being locked up in an attic for fifteen years out of eighteen meant I didn't always follow the nuances of conversations and the unspoken messages. I would ask Jack later what she meant.

"So you can't think of anyone he might stay with in

Hertfordshire?" Jack asked Mrs. Dodd.

She shook her head. "Of course he may have rented a place under an assumed name. That horrible Hamley, for example."

"What do you know of him?"

"Very little. He came to live with Mr. Tate only a few weeks ago. I suspected they were, uh...you know." She blushed fiercely and sipped her sherry.

Jack and Samuel looked down at their ales. I was left to stare at them all in turn. Was she implying that Tate and Ham were lovers? Surely not. They were both men. So...how did that work? None of the biology texts smuggled in by my tutor at Windamere had covered that topic.

I was contemplating the answer when Jack cleared his throat. "If you've been with Tate for so long, you must know August Langley, my uncle."

"Yes, of course." She made a face. "I can't say I was sorry to see him leave. He wasn't a bad man, but the two of them together was not a happy mix. They argued a lot, mostly over their work."

"Do you know how he lost the use of his legs?" I asked.

"It happened in a fire. The same fire that cost Mr. Tate his arm."

"How awful."

"It was. They both nearly died."

"Do you know how the fire started?" Jack asked.

"It was an accident with Mr. Tate's chemicals, so he said. There were a lot of fires in those days, all started the same way. Chemistry is a dangerous business, but they were trying to do good things with it. Mr. Tate has developed some wonderful cures for all sorts of ailments. I'm very proud of him." Her eyes clouded and she looked down at her glass. "Or I was. So why does he want you specifically, Miss Smith? Does it have something to do with your name?"

"My name?" I rubbed my temple where a headache hammered my skull.

"What about her name?" Jack asked.

"Hannah Smith. I recognized it, but couldn't place it until after you left earlier. Then I remembered. It was a name I heard repeatedly many years ago."

"Eighteen years?" Samuel asked.

"Oh no, longer than that. It was very soon after I began working for them."

"That can't be right," I said. "I'm eighteen."

Mrs. Dodd shook her head. "It couldn't have been you. The other Miss Smith was an adult. Perhaps you were named after her."

"Who was she?" I asked.

"I don't know and I never met her. Mr. Tate and Mr. Langley mentioned her name often, which is why it's stayed in my mind all this time. Their discussions concerning her were sometimes heated, but they always ended them when I walked into the room. I thought perhaps they were rivals for her affections, but back then I didn't know about...you know."

"Could she have been somebody they worked with?" Jack asked. "Another scientist?"

Or someone they experimented upon?

"Perhaps," Mrs. Dodd said. "I don't know what happened to her. They stopped talking about her after a while. I hadn't heard the name in years until you turned up. Do you think your parents knew her?"

"I never knew my parents," I said. "All I do know is that Mr. Langley and Mr. Tate took care of me when I was a baby."

She gasped. "Oh! My! I remember you!" She pressed a hand to her breast and stared at me in wonder. "I'm so happy to see you again, dear. So happy. You cannot begin to know how relieved I am that you've turned out well. Look at you. What a beauty. And red hair too. You had none then. Completely bald, you were."

My heart swelled unexpectedly. I didn't remember her, but clearly she remembered me and had worried for me. Her reaction connected me to her, and I felt lucky that someone had cared enough to be happy to see me again.

"What about Jack?" I asked.

"You mean Mr. Langley here?" She shrugged. "What about him?"

"He lived with Langley and Tate as a baby a few years before me. Do you remember that?"

"Oh yes, of course I remember a baby. You mean to say *this* Mr. Langley is *that* baby?" Her eyes brightened then filled with tears. She clasped her hands over her mouth. "My goodness. I can't believe it. I simply can't believe it. To find both of you after all this time is wonderful. A miracle."

Jack looked a little unnerved by her reaction, but he managed a smile. "How did I come to be in the household?"

"Your arrival was most strange. I'm not even sure how they got you. Mr. Langley simply came home with you one day and said you were given to him to care for. Do you mean to say you're his nephew?"

"So he told me," Jack said quietly.

"Now that is a surprise. I didn't even know he had family. He never told me. You don't look like him either. I do remember you though, Mr. Langley. And you too, Miss Smith. He was gone by the time you came along, though. Both orphans, you were. Poor things. You were both lucky they took you in, or so I thought at first. I often wondered what happened to you." She bit her wobbly lip and gave us a watery smile. "It warms my heart to see you both again."

"Tell me what you knew of Jack as a baby."

She sipped her sherry and frowned. "Nothing really. He was a sweet little thing. You both were. Then again, I always did have a soft spot for babies. They wouldn't let me near either of you though. You had nurses, and you were mostly kept in the nursery."

"Why did Jack leave?" I asked. "And where did he go?"

"Ah." Her face darkened and she glanced at Jack. "That was my fault. It was the fires, you see. There were so many at that time, and I feared for his life. He was so little and the experiments Mr. Tate and Mr. Langley were conducting were extremely volatile. The nursery adjoined their laboratory, and I begged them to move the baby to a safer room, but they refused. In the end, I informed the authorities of the danger and they took him away. He was sent to an orphanage and then a family adopted him. I didn't know he was Langley's nephew," she muttered. "Good lord, I wonder why he never said."

Probably because he wasn't related to Jack at all.

"Did you ever hear about me again?" Jack asked.

She shook her head. "Both Langley and Tate tried to find you for a while. They never did, nor did they learn of my involvement, thank goodness. I would have lost my position, and I did like working for them. They were kind and generous for the most part."

"What about when I arrived?" I asked.

"By then the fires weren't as frequent, although they still occurred from time to time. You weren't there for long anyway," she said.

"What of my parents? Mr. Langley told me my father died in one of the factories and my mother died soon after putting me in their care."

"That's right. Terrible business, it was. That poor woman. She was desperate. I knew her a little. Our husbands had worked together before Mr. Dodd died. When she came to the house, I promised her I'd look after you, and so did Mr. Langley and Mr. Tate. I was shocked when Mr. Langley informed me one day that he'd given you away to a nice family. Shocked and a little saddened, but I knew in my heart it was best for you. Were they kind to you?"

"They were." I saw no reason to tell her otherwise. Her life had been sad enough. There was no reason to add the burden of my confinement to it.

"Mr. Tate was shocked too," she went on. "Indeed, he was furious and ranted for days. He searched everywhere for you, but to no avail. Mr. Langley refused to tell him where you'd gone, and I didn't know either. Mr. Tate never really gave up looking for you entirely. He employed private enquiry agents all over the country, but none found you. I began to think he'd cared for you like a father, he was so persistent. And now you say he's trying to kidnap you. How awful. I still find what he did in the factory a few weeks ago quite unfathomable. I admit that I don't understand him at all."

"His mind isn't right," I said. There simply was no other explanation for it without going into details.

"Indeed it's not." She shook her head. "He's changed dramatically these past few months."

"In what way?" Jack asked.

"Ever since he found out he was dying—"

"Dying!" the three of us said as one.

"Oh yes. Didn't you know? He told me so himself. Ever since then he's been like a man possessed, trying to cure himself. It's all he thinks about."

"Dying?" I frowned. "What from?"

She shrugged. "He never told me. But I noticed him getting more and more tired, and he seemed to always have a fever. He was burning up. Couldn't you tell?"

My heart ground to a halt. I looked to Jack. He stared back at me. Samuel too. I could feel their eyes on me even when I looked down at my hands resting on the table. My hot hands. I swallowed the lump in my throat, but another replaced it. My face heated. Exhaustion clawed at me, trying to drag me down.

Tate was dying, and if I had to guess, I'd say he was dying from the fire within him. It was consuming him. Growing hotter and hotter, drawing on his energy. He'd infected himself with the fire years ago, and now he was paying the price for his desire to be powerful. A much higher price than not being able to control it when he grew angry.

He had infected me with the same compound.

I was dying too.

CHAPTER 12

"Are you all right, Miss Smith?" Mrs. Dodd said. "You look quite flushed all of a sudden."

I stared at her. My heart hurt. My mouth was dry. I felt heavy, as if I would sink through the chair and disappear into the floor.

Dying.

"Jack," I whispered.

He must have made the connection too. He reached across the table, but his fingers curled up into a ball before he touched me. "Hannah." The green of his eyes darkened and a muscle high up in his jaw clenched. His lips formed the word 'no' and he shook his head over and over as he stared at me. As if the harder he stared, the better I'd feel and it would turn out that nothing was wrong with me after all.

Yet he could not will me to be well. I knew with complete certainty that death had wrapped its arms around me and was pulling me to its breast.

Samuel cleared his throat. "She's had a long day."

"You need an early night," Mrs. Dodd said. "Take some laudanum and go to bed early."

"Thank you," Samuel said when I failed to answer.

Mrs. Dodd checked the small pocket watch she kept in her reticule. "I must go. Thank you for the drink. It was nice to meet you two again after all this time." She looked first to Jack then to me. He didn't seem to notice, he was still staring at me. "Just lovely to see you both grown up and looking well."

I think I managed to say something in response. I don't know. I wasn't fully aware of everything. Just that I felt so hot and tired, and that Jack appeared stricken. Did I look like that too?

Samuel stood and thanked Mrs. Dodd for coming. He seemed to be the only one of us capable of speaking.

"Do be careful, Miss Smith," Mrs. Dodd said and waved goodbye.

Once she was gone, Samuel sat back down. "Don't even think it," he said. "Just because Tate is dying doesn't mean Hannah is."

Jack looked up and nodded. "You're right, Gladstone, for once." His eyes were bright and hard, his mouth a determined line. "We won't jump to conclusions yet."

If it made him happier to believe that, then so be it. But I knew. I knew in my heart, my soul and in my hot blood. I was dying from the fire Tate had injected into me, and there was no cure.

I spread my hands on the tabletop to steady myself. I felt unbalanced, like I was spinning, or perhaps the room was. Jack watched me intently, his gaze making me hotter.

"Hannah..." The ache in his voice cut through me.

I closed my eyes. Breathed. Opened them again. "Samuel's right," I said more cheerfully than I felt. "Tate's situation and mine are different."

Jack said nothing. His moment of fortitude had vanished entirely. It had been brief and not altogether convincing anyway. He clutched his tankard between both hands and gazed at the golden ale.

"Good." Samuel gave an emphatic nod, as if he'd made a

decision that I was well and that was that. "So why do you think Hannah was named after the other Hannah Smith? And who was she?"

"And is she linked to Jack in some way?" I said. "What do you think, Jack?"

He drained the rest of his ale. "I think I need another drink. Something stronger." He went to get up, but Samuel grabbed his forearm and pulled him back to the seat.

"Don't," Samuel said.

"I'll drink if I bloody well want to."

"Jack," I pleaded.

He raked his hand through his hair and turned his face away from us. His breathing became shallow and quick, his shoulders hunched. Samuel looked to me and I saw the concern in his eyes, and the uncertainty. He was at a loss for what to say and do.

"Jack?" I said.

He pressed his thumb and finger into his eyes and a shudder wracked him. His other hand reached across the table to me, but of course I didn't take it. God how I wanted to. I ached for his touch.

"Try and get through the meeting with Culvert before falling apart," Samuel said to him. "Can you do that?"

"I need you to be strong," I added.

He looked at me. Misery streaked through his eyes, shadowed his jaw, tugged at his mouth. He sucked in two deep breaths then finally nodded. "We'd better go then." His voice shook and he cleared his throat again. "Come on."

We drove to George Culvert's house in silence. Samuel was outside on the driver's seat while Jack remained in the cabin with me. Neither of us spoke. It was as if talking about it would somehow make it more real. He sat opposite me and leaned forward, his elbows resting on his knees, his hands very close to mine.

I stared out the window, but it was dark, and I wasn't really concentrating anyway. Thousands of thoughts and questions raced through my mind. Was I really dying? Could

I be cured? Should I see a doctor? There were no answers, of course. The questions became more jumbled up and tangled as the glowing gas lamps slipped by.

"We'll have an early night," Jack said when we arrived at the Culvert residence. "You need to rest."

Rest would not come easily to me now. There were too many questions, too many things to think about. Too much to do.

How much time did I have left?

The butler showed us into the parlor where a pregnant Mrs. Culvert and her husband greeted us.

"Forgive us, we're poor company tonight," I said after initial polite chatter came to an abrupt stop.

"Of course," Mrs. Culvert said. "You've been traveling and have a lot on your minds."

She had no idea.

"Dinner will be served soon. George, perhaps you ought to give them the incantation now, so you don't forget." She laughed and it was so good to hear. She was a delightful lady, very handsome and fair. The only resemblance between her and her brother, Jacob Beaufort, was their bright blue eyes. Hers sparkled at her husband as he fished in his pocket.

"Here it is." Mr. Culvert gave a piece of paper to Jack. "Memorize it and say the words in the presence of the demon. Ensure you also have the amulet on you. Keep it in your pocket at all times."

"Do you have any more thoughts on why it may have been summoned?" Samuel asked.

Mr. Culvert shook his head. "It's not for doing good, I can assure you that much."

"What about the dungeon? How did it get in there?"

"I think it accidentally ended up in the dungeon instead of where the summoner intended. Recently too I might add."

"Why?"

"It wouldn't have survived any length of time after consuming the spirits if it couldn't escape. It requires ongoing sustenance. Perhaps a few days at the most."

Jack and Samuel exchanged a worried glance.

"You already know someone capable of summoning a demon and intent on doing you harm," Mr. Culvert said. "Do you think it was him?"

"Who?" Mrs. Culvert asked, slowly rubbing her belly. "What happened?"

Her husband pushed his glasses up his nose. "I was going to tell you when, uh, your nerves were stronger."

"My nerves are perfectly all right, thank you, George. Don't force me to ask Emily. You know she'll tell me. Unlike you, she doesn't think me weak."

"I don't think you weak. Merely..." He colored and looked away.

"Female," she finished for him. She rolled her eyes. "Miss Smith, do you find men underestimate your strength?"

"On occasion," I said and tried to smile.

"There is a man after Miss Smith here," Mr. Culvert told his wife. "He made himself known when we were at Frakingham. Never fear, we frightened him off."

She bit her lip and blinked at her husband. Despite her teasing, she was clearly worried about him. "That's awful," she murmured.

"It may have been Tate who summoned it," Jack said. "He's certainly capable."

"So the incantation will be enough to send it back?" Samuel asked. "I don't want to chant it and find the demon doesn't respond."

"It will. Just make sure you're holding the amulet." Mr. Culvert sighed. "There are a lot of rules in this business. My life would be a great deal easier if I owned a blade forged in the Otherworld."

"I'm not sure my nerves would be any happier," Mrs. Culvert said. "You're very good with books and theories, George, but weapons aren't really your specialty."

He laughed. She smiled too and patted her large belly.

"If it must be held by someone," Jack said, "and I found that amulet in the trench, half buried in the soil...I wonder if the builder summoned it."

"The one who died?" I asked. "It seems possible. He was the closest to the dungeon, but there were others."

"Two more builders and Yardley the foreman."

"He was the one who alerted us," I said. "I doubt it was him."

"And the other two builders seemed absolutely terrified," Samuel said. "The one who died was the only person showing no real fear."

"He was more curious that anything," Jack agreed.

"Why would he want to summon a demon?" I asked.

Mr. Culvert pushed his glasses up his nose. "Perhaps a more apt question would be who paid him to do it?"

***

The journey home to Frakingham seemed to take forever. I slept part of the way as Jack drove and Samuel kept him company. I suspected they'd left me so that I could rest, but despite the odd nap here and there, sleep remained elusive. A sense of numb disbelief had settled over me and that helped distance me from the facts.

Finally we arrived back at the house in the late afternoon. It was quiet. Too quiet. No one greeted us. No faces appeared at the windows.

I opened the carriage door myself and hopped out without letting the step down. Jack and Samuel looked to one another then scanned the area.

"Something's wrong," I said.

"We'll take the horses to the stables," Jack said. "All of us together."

I climbed up beside them onto the driver's seat and Jack drove the horses round to the back of the house. The men unhitched the carriage and settled the horses in their stalls with feed. They needed more care before nightfall, but that would have to wait. We had to find out where everyone had gone.

Dread gnawed at me. The hairs on the back of my neck stood up and despite the ever-present heat within, a shiver trickled down my spine. We crossed the courtyard and entered the house.

"Hello?" Samuel called. The shout bounced between the archways and walls. No one answered.

We stood. Waited. I wasn't sure whether to check the bedrooms first, the parlor, or the kitchen area, so instead I did nothing. None of us moved. It was as if taking a step in one direction would shatter the hope we all still held onto.

"It *is* you!" Sylvia cried.

I looked up the stairs to see her running down them.

"Oh, thank God." She was crying and running, almost tripping over her skirts. She ran straight into Jack's arms and sobbed into his chest.

"Shhh," he whispered. "Calm yourself, Syl. Tell us what happened."

My heart thudded once then ground to a halt. *Oh God.* I put my hand to her back. "Sylvia," I said gently. "Talk to us."

She pulled away from Jack and clutched my hand. Samuel offered her a handkerchief and she wiped her eyes. They were swollen from crying.

"Tommy?" Jack muttered. His face was ravaged with shadows and lines. It had been like that all day. He'd not slept a wink and now this.

Sylvia shook her head. "Olsen." A fresh bout of tears streamed down her cheeks. "He's dead."

I pressed a hand to my stomach as tears pricked my eyes. Sylvia drew me into a fierce hug, her damp cheeks against mine.

"It was awful," she said. "Just awful. The demon got him."

"Ham?" Samuel asked.

"The other one."

"Where's Tommy?" Jack asked. "Why isn't he here? And the other servants and August, where are they?"

"The servants have all been dismissed and are safe in the village. Uncle is in his rooms with Bollard, and Tommy is upstairs in his bedroom. I've just come from there."

She'd been alone with a male servant in his room? Sylvia would never do that. Something must be very wrong.

"What's happened to him?" Jack asked, urgent. "Is he...?"

"He's injured," she said.

"Yes, we know," Samuel said. "He hurt his leg before we left."

She shook her head. "It got him again. He tried to save Olsen, but couldn't. The demon struck him in the shoulder." She started crying again. "There was blood everywhere."

Jack raced up the stairs and was soon gone from sight. I would let him talk to Tommy for a few minutes before I joined them.

"Has a doctor seen him?" Samuel asked.

"It's too dangerous to get one up here. I've tended to his wounds myself."

"Your uncle?" I asked. "Is he all right?"

"The same as always. Bollard too. It's just been the four of us here since we sent the servants away yesterday after..." She drew in a shuddery breath. "After Olsen was attacked."

"How did it happen?"

"Olsen and Tommy went to feed the horses, and the demon came out of the woods. It was so fast." She pressed her fingers to her mouth and shook her head. "They both had fire and guns, but it didn't seem as frightened of them this time. Tommy actually burned it and that sent it scurrying, but before that, it didn't seem to care."

"Perhaps it's learned that bullets can't kill it," I said.

"Oh, Hannah," she whispered. "Poor Olsen."

I hugged her again until she calmed, then Samuel and I went upstairs to Tommy's room while Sylvia went to fetch her uncle. Tommy sat on top of the bedcovers, the bandaged shoulder clearly visible beneath his white shirt. He wore no waistcoat or jacket, and he held his arm stiffly against his body.

"I'm very glad to see you three," he said with a glance at the door. "Miss Langley needs your company, Miss Smith."

"Driving you mad is she?" Jack asked, attempting to be light.

"She fusses and won't let me get up to do my duty."

"You're injured!" I cried.

"I still have one good arm."

"For Heaven's sake, Tommy, enjoy the peace while you can. You deserve a rest."

"Not sure how much peace he's getting up here with Sylvia mothering him," Jack said. "Or should that be smothering."

"She does talk a lot," Tommy said with a small smile. "But she's good company. When she's not crying."

She entered the room then, Bollard and Langley behind her. "I thought I heard your arrival," Langley said to us. "Why didn't you come to see me immediately?"

"We heard about Tommy," Jack said.

"As you can see, he's well enough. He should be working. With the rest of the staff gone, there's a lot to do."

"I agree, sir," Tommy said.

"No!" Sylvia cried, stamping a hand on her hip. "You need to rest. There'll be no more talk of you getting out of bed until you're healed. We can manage without you."

I had to commend her. I hadn't expected Sylvia to rise to the challenge of doing servants' work. It would seem she wasn't as spoiled as she appeared, although I wasn't looking forward to dinner.

"Well done, Syl," Jack said. He looked at his cousin as if he'd never quite seen her before. "You've kept everything in order in our absence. It hasn't been easy for you."

Langley grunted. "We'll speak later, Sylvia. Jack, tell us what you learned in London. We need to get rid of this creature, and Tate too. We can't live like this for much longer. You'll all go mad."

The use of 'you' and not 'we' wasn't lost on me. Did he not include himself because he was already mad?

There wasn't a lot of space in Tommy's room, so Sylvia sat on the chair beside the bed while I sat on the bed itself.

Jack, Samuel and Bollard remained standing. Jack told them about the incantation and everything Culvert had instructed us to do, as well as our thoughts on who had summoned it.

"Tate is the most likely suspect," Langley said.

"He could have paid the builder to speak the words and hold the amulet," I said.

Langley nodded. "We need to find out more about the man and who his associates were. Once the demon is caught and returned, you can venture into the village and speak to his widow. She may be able to identify Tate."

"If it wasn't Tate, then who?" Samuel asked.

We all looked to Langley. He shrugged.

"Not even a suspicion?"

His only answer was a sharp glare.

"In the meantime," Sylvia said, "we have Ham to contend with too." She rubbed her arms and looked to her cousin. "When will it end?"

"Soon, Syl. Don't worry, we're all set with the incantation."

"What did Mrs. Dodd say?" Langley asked.

Jack glanced at me. "She doesn't know how to find Tate. She did give us a clue as to why Tate is desperate to get Hannah though."

Langley leaned forward. "Go on."

"He's dying. We suspect the fire inside him is killing him somehow."

"Dying?" Sylvia said. "Well, that's good news. I wonder how long he has."

Nobody else spoke. Langley turned to me, his mouth slightly ajar, his face pale. Tommy eventually looked at me too. They'd made the connection.

"What?" Sylvia said, frowning. "Why are you all staring at Hannah?"

Part of me didn't want to tell her. She would be happier in her ignorance.

"Well?"

"If Tate is dying from the fire, then it means Hannah may

be too," Langley said.

Sylvia sat very still for a few moments. Then she shrugged and snorted. "No. Don't be absurd. Look at her. She's a picture of health. A little flushed and tired from her journey, but that's all. She cannot be dying. You're wrong, Uncle. You all are." She crossed her arms and lifted her chin.

"We need to find a cure," Jack said to Langley, his tone urgent. "Set aside whatever you're working on. This takes priority."

"A cure *is* what I've been working on," he snapped.

Jack blinked at him. "What do you mean?"

"I've been looking for a cure for you."

"Me?"

"Of course."

"But…why?"

Langley shrugged one shoulder. Behind him, Bollard shifted his weight from one foot to the other, but it was the only movement he made. Not even his eyes blinked. "The why isn't important," Langley said. I disagreed, but he continued to speak, not letting anyone else get a word in. "I don't know if I'm close, but I've been making progress. The cure was intended for you all along, but it should benefit Hannah too."

"How close are you to finishing it?" Jack asked.

Langley's gaze slipped to his tightly clasped hands in his lap.

"August!" Jack shouted. "Answer me. How close are you?"

"Not as close as I'd like." He looked up at me. "I'll be honest with you, Hannah. You do indeed look hotter and more tired. You need this cure soon, and it has all come as an immense surprise to me. If I'd known Reuben was dying, I could have worked harder. I'm sorry." His eyes closed and he shook his head. "I'm so sorry."

I curled my fingers into the bedcovers and hung on. Everything was tilting and sliding: the room, the furniture….me. It was so surreal and didn't seem normal to hear Langley apologizing to me. He sounded sincere and worried. Like he cared. His frequent mood changes weren't my biggest concern, however. Not now.

"It's all right," I heard myself say.

"It's not bloody all right!" Jack shouted. He stood over his uncle, his fists glowing at his sides. "You *have* to cure her. Do you understand me! You have to find a cure or I'll…" The end of his sentence was lost in a choke. He strode out of the room, slamming the door behind him.

I rose and followed.

CHAPTER 13

I searched everywhere and eventually found Jack sitting in the window seat in my bedroom. He sat side-on, his knees drawn up, his elbow resting on them and his cheek in his hand. I pulled a chair over and sat down. I placed my hand near him on the seat, as close as I dared. I was so hot that touching him would have emitted an enormous spark and swell the fire in me to a dangerous level.

"Jack, look at me," I said gently.

He lowered his hand and turned. His eyes were red and swollen, his jaw clenched hard. His body was rigid and tight, as if he were holding himself together with sheer force of will. He rested his hand next to mine. Heat surged inside me, but I didn't move away. I needed the comfort of being close, and I suspected he needed it even more.

"It'll be all right," I said. "Have faith."

He closed his eyes and expelled a long breath. "It's hard," he muttered.

"I know. But we have to believe I'll be cured. *You* have to believe it. If you don't, then it makes it even harder for me to have hope. Understand?"

He opened his eyes and gave a slight nod. I didn't think

his doubts and fears had miraculously disappeared, but it was a start. "You're a remarkable woman, Hannah Smith. I wish I had half as much courage as you."

I didn't feel courageous or strong, just desperate and so very scared. At least I knew now that I wasn't alone. "Langley is the foremost microbiologist in the country," I teased. "Perhaps the world. He can do this."

That almost raised a smile from him. "I do agree that if someone will find a cure, it'll be him."

"You had no idea he was looking for a cure for you?"

He shook his head. "I'm stunned. He never gave any indication. I'm not even sure why he's trying. As far as I'm concerned, there's nothing wrong with me. I can control the fire."

"I agree," I said with a smile. "There's nothing wrong with you."

"No? So you don't think I'm stubborn? Temperamental?"

"Yes, but those traits are ones I can live with."

"Not everyone finds them as insignificant as you."

"Are you talking about Miss Charity? Because I warn you, I'll grow jealous."

"Really? You're jealous of her?" He leaned forward, his mouth very close to mine. His breath fanned my lips. "You don't need to be. Anyone who can put up with me like you do deserves my undying devotion."

I pushed him in the shoulder and received a shock up my arm for my carelessness. I jerked back.

Jack pulled away. "Are you hurt?"

"No," I said, rubbing my hand where a tingling sensation lingered. "But I should be more careful."

"Do you feel hotter?"

"A little." I felt a *lot* hotter, but I didn't want to worry him. "I want to speak to Langley," I said. "We haven't told him everything Mrs. Dodd said."

"There are a lot of unanswered questions, but I'm not sure now is a good time."

"You think we should leave him alone to work?"

He nodded. "Nothing should distract him."

"But I've just discovered he has a heart after all. I thought we could ask him about you and me as babies. Come on, Jack. I know you want to know as much as I do. We'll be quick."

He gave me a grim smile. "I'm not very good at saying no to you."

We walked together down the hall to Langley's rooms. Bollard opened the door and Langley sat at his desk, bent over a ledger filled with densely scrawled figures.

"What is it?" he asked, gruff. Any sympathy and concern he'd showed earlier was gone. He was back to being the Langley I knew, but now I wondered if that was a mask. Why he wore one, I couldn't say.

"There are some things we need to know," Jack said.

"Ah. Mrs. Dodd. I was wondering when you were going to bring her up. I thought perhaps you'd forgotten what with all Hannah's problems."

"It's something of a diversion for us right now," I said. "Why did you let us look for her knowing she may say certain things you didn't want discovered?"

"Perhaps a better question would be, why didn't you just tell us everything in the first place?" Jack snapped. "Well?"

"I let you go for precisely the reason I gave at the time— she was our only link to Tate, albeit a tenuous one. It was necessary that you speak to her and learn what you could about his whereabouts. I admit that I'd hoped neither of you would connect her to your own pasts, but it seems you did. Indeed, I wasn't even sure you'd find her. If the police couldn't, how did you?"

"The last known address that Weeks gave us was where her sister worked," Jack said. "She knew where Mrs. Dodd had gone, although she was reluctant to tell us or the police. Gladstone persuaded her."

Langley's gaze switched to Bollard, still standing behind me at the door. I turned, but Bollard's face was blank.

Jack pressed his knuckles on the desk and leaned over.

"Give us some answers, August."

"I will," Langley conceded with a nod.

"Mrs. Dodd told us about baby Hannah and baby Jack, although neither of us had names then. She also told us about Hannah's namesake. Who was the original Hannah Smith?"

"A friend of Wade's."

Of all the possible things I'd considered, that wasn't one of them. "Did he name me Hannah Smith in memory of her?"

"I've never spoken to him about it," he said. "I only learned your name when you told us yourself upon arriving here. I suspect you were named after her, though."

"Why?" Jack asked. "What significance does she have?"

"They were good friends."

"Lovers?"

Langley shrugged. "You'd have to ask him that."

"Mrs. Dodd said she heard you and Tate arguing about Hannah Smith," Jack said. "Why?"

"She…she was the sort of person men argued over."

Now *that* certainly wasn't the answer I'd expected to hear in light of what Mrs. Dodd had told us about Tate's preference for men over women. Perhaps she'd been mistaken. Or perhaps Langley was being deliberately evasive. Again.

"How did I come to live with you?" Jack asked him.

"Your father gave you to me."

"Your brother?" I asked.

He lifted his gaze to mine then turned it on Jack. "No. You're not my nephew, but I suspect you already knew that."

Jack sat heavily in a chair near the desk. Like me, he probably hadn't expected an honest answer. "I suspected. Who is my father?"

"That's not important."

"It is to me."

He glanced past me to Bollard. I turned and saw the mute signing something with his hands. When he finished, he let them drop to his sides again. His expression hadn't changed. Langley shook his head, but whether it was in response to Bollard or Jack, I wasn't sure.

"Your father doesn't want you to know," Langley said. "He swore me to secrecy, and I will oblige him."

I heard Bollard move behind me, but when I turned to look he seemed to be in exactly the same position, with exactly the same bland expression on his face. I wasn't sure how any of this affected him, but he seemed far more animated in this conversation than I'd ever seen him before.

Jack sat back in his chair and shook his head slowly. "I can't believe you won't tell me."

"I'm sorry," Langley said. "It's not my wish, but his."

I went to stand beside Jack and rested my hand on the arm of his chair to offer some measure of comfort. "Why did his father bring Jack to you?"

"He thought we could cure him of the fire."

"But you couldn't."

Jack rose and indicated I should take the chair. I sat and watched Langley closely. So far he seemed mostly unmoved by the conversation and a little distracted. Perhaps what he'd just learned about me was playing on his mind.

"Mrs. Dodd said the authorities took me away," Jack said, skirting the role she'd had in the event. "How did you find me again?"

"I searched everywhere, and eventually learned you'd been adopted by a family. The Cutlers. They were nice people. Normal. I watched them with you on outings. They seemed to care for you and you looked happy. I never once saw your fire, and there was only the one report of a blaze at their residence in those years. So I left you with them and never returned. I believe they died when you were two or three."

"I don't remember them. What happened to me?"

He shrugged. "The Cutlers had no family to take you in. Perhaps you were put into an orphanage, or maybe you just slipped through the system. It happens. If I'd known they'd died, I would have come for you myself."

"Why *did* you come looking for me eight years ago?"

"I heard a strange story about a boy who could shoot fire from his fingers just by pointing. I hired enquiry agents and they found you. I knew you were my friend's boy when I heard the name Cutler."

"So you took him back in," I said. It was quite a remarkable story. Not that Langley had found him, but that he'd searched for him. Worried about him. Wanted him to be happy with real parents and no fire. I was very much in danger of believing Langley truly did care.

"Don't think anything sentimental about it, Hannah," Langley said, bursting my happy bubble. "He was a danger to others. When he was a baby, he couldn't control the fire. He was much too young. It wasn't until he came to live with me later that I realized he could now that he'd grown."

"Well, that in itself is reason to think you're a kind man, Mr. Langley. No matter how cantankerous you pretend to be, I no longer believe it."

"Don't jump to conclusions too soon," Jack muttered.

Behind me, I could swear Bollard made a noise that could have been either a laugh or a grunt or just a clearing of his throat.

"This isn't a joke," Langley said. "Now, if you don't mind, I have work to do."

"Just one more thing," Jack said, rising. "The compound that Tate injected into himself to give him the fire, did it come from me?"

Langley nodded.

I gasped. "You let him do that to a baby?"

"I didn't *let* him do anything, Hannah. He just did it. Rest assured, Jack wasn't harmed. A few pricks here and there to test his blood, then a needle in the arm. He probably screamed for a few seconds until it was out. I don't know. Reuben only conducted his experiments when I wasn't there. He knew my thoughts on the matter didn't align with his."

"It sounds awful," I muttered.

"*Now* will you two leave me in peace?"

We left, and as I passed Bollard, I noticed him watching Jack with a strange expression. It wasn't blank, as usual, but it was difficult to decipher nevertheless. Curiosity perhaps.

"What do you think of that?" I asked Jack as we walked along the corridor.

"I think he still hasn't told us everything."

"No, but it's a start."

"I wish I knew who my real parents were."

"Do you think he'll ever tell you?"

"No." He glanced over his shoulder back the way we'd come. "But that doesn't mean I can't find out some other way."

"How?"

"Don't worry about it," he said.

I stopped. "You're going to break into his rooms? Jack!"

"Shhh. Hannah, I have to find out. I hate not knowing." He held up his hands and wiggled his fingers. "This must have come from one of them."

"And what if you find out something about them you don't like? He already said your father didn't want to be known to you. Perhaps there's a good reason for that and not knowing is better."

"I don't care. There may not be any records of my parents anyway, but I have to try to find out." He strode off. I sighed and watched him go.

"Remember how I said your stubbornness doesn't trouble me?" I called after him, hands on hips. "I take it back."

He turned around and grinned as he walked back. "Dearest Hannah, you wound me."

"If I could touch you, I'd thump you right now."

"And if I could touch you, I'd..." He sighed. "Never mind. Those thoughts are best left unsaid otherwise I'll need to go for a swim."

I fanned my heating face with my hand. "I'm beginning to think I need to learn how to swim too."

***

Dinner was indeed an interesting affair. Fortunately the cook had prepared a day's worth of food for us, but Sylvia still needed to warm it up in the oven. She enlisted Jack's help but wouldn't let Tommy or me into the kitchen. We both needed to rest, apparently. I sat in Tommy's room with Samuel until Jack fetched us when dinner was ready.

"What are you both doing?" he said with a frown at us. "Gladstone, you're not helping. They should both be resting."

"You sound like Sylvia," I said.

That only deepened his frown. "It's not a joke, Hannah."

"No amount of rest is going to cure me."

His face twisted. His eyes darkened. He spun round and stalked off down the corridor. I raced after him.

"Slow down," I called. He opened the door leading to the main part of the house, but didn't go through, nor did he turn around.

"Jack, I…" I didn't know what to say. I wasn't sorry for attempting to take everybody's mind off the facts. "I need you all to be as normal as possible."

"Normal," he bit off. "How can I pretend as if nothing's wrong?" He leaned his forehead against the door. "I'm losing you, Hannah. You're slipping away from me and I can't…I can't be without you. I just can't."

His words shocked me to the core. I knew he cared for me, but this…it was more than I'd ever hoped for. He was handsome and strong, caring and capable. I was just a freckly redhead who'd spent most of her life in an attic and set things on fire without meaning to. Yet *this* man harbored deep feelings for me.

"I can't even hold you," he murmured so quietly I almost missed it.

I moved up behind him, but it took all my strength not to wrap my arms around his waist and press my cheek to his back.

"One day you will," I said. "Langley will find a cure."

He raked both hands through his hair, down his face, and lowered his head. His shoulders shook. If only I could flatten my palms to them and lend him some of the certainty I felt in Langley's abilities. I hovered very close, but soon even that became too much, too hot. I stepped back.

It was a long time before he spoke again. "We'd better go down to dinner."

"Yes. Sylvia won't be happy if she's gone to all that trouble, and we don't eat."

He turned around, a weak smile on his lips that wasn't reflected at all in his miserable eyes. He indicated I should walk ahead of him, and I passed through the door. The heat inside me roared to life, and I gasped as a spark shot from my fingers. I stamped it out where it landed.

"You really shouldn't speak to me with such tenderness," I teased. "It's rather dangerous."

"I know," he said, tugging his collar. "I'm burning up inside."

We met Sylvia and Samuel in the dining room and discussed how to hunt the demon. Nobody would allow Jack to go on his own and that meant Samuel had to go with him. They settled on an early morning start.

"What about Bollard?" I asked. "He could join you. Three is better than two."

"I'll ask August later if he can spare him," Jack said.

"Tell me what Mrs. Dodd was like," Sylvia said, ladling soup into Jack's bowl. She'd taken it upon herself to serve everyone the first course, and I admit to being surprised that she hadn't complained once.

"She was lovely." I stared down at my soup. "It was nice to know that she'd cared for us as babies. She worried about Tate and Langley too. She seemed fond of them both and quite sad that Tate has turned out the way he has."

"I did find her observation about Tate a little...odd," Samuel said.

"What observation?" Sylvia asked. She set down the soup tureen on the sideboard and joined us at the table.

Samuel, Jack and I exchanged glances.

"Out with it," she prompted. "I refuse to be kept in the dark."

Both men suddenly filled their mouths with soup, so it was left to me. "She implied that he liked male company."

"That's not terribly surprising. A lot of men do. Look at the proliferation of gentlemen-only clubs."

"She wasn't referring to their friendship," I said, my face heating. It was, after all, not the sort of conversation one should have at the dinner table, or indeed anywhere.

Sylvia dropped her spoon, splashing pea and ham soup onto the tablecloth. "Good lord! You mean he's...*fond* of men. Isn't that illegal?"

"Is it?" I asked.

Jack nodded. "Tate's lucky she never gave his secret away."

Good lord. I had no idea.

"Well." Sylvia picked up her spoon. "That puts a different light on things. Obviously he was already warped before he injected himself with the fire."

"There's no evidence to suggest that," Samuel said. "Whether he was born that way or came to it later in life, the science isn't clear."

"Perhaps it's not something that can be scientifically explained," I said. "Love generally isn't."

"Love!" Sylvia scoffed. "Who's speaking of love?"

I concentrated on my soup in order to hide my pink cheeks. I admit that intimacy of that nature was an unfamiliar topic to me. I thought love and passion went together. After all, I felt both for Jack. But perhaps in others that wasn't how it worked. I felt completely inadequate to talk about it and wished the topic would change altogether.

Samuel cleared his throat. "I think you and I should watch over Hannah tonight, Langley."

I gave him a nod of thanks and he smiled back.

"Agreed," Jack said. He pointed his spoon at Sylvia. "Not a word from you about it being improper to be in her room."

"I didn't say a thing! I actually think it's a good idea. Perhaps we shouldn't tell Uncle though. And another thing."

"What is it?" Jack asked.

"May I come in too?"

I grinned. "Of course. Perhaps Tommy—"

"No. I draw the line at having him with us. Besides, Tate knows you won't be sleeping in the servants' wing. He won't send Ham in there. Tommy'll be quite safe where he is."

"Perhaps I should sleep in the servants' wing too then," I said.

"Good idea," Jack said. "Well done, Syl."

She beamed. "Thank you. I'd wager you didn't expect me to come up with a good idea."

"Yet again, you're right. Oh look, pigs are flying past the window."

She gave him a withering glare. "Very amusing."

After dinner we made up the beds in one of the servants' rooms. Since two of the maids slept together, it had a large bed, but the room itself was quite small. The men decided they only needed one extra mattress as one of them would always be awake to keep watch.

It was only early, but I felt so tired that I retired for the night. Jack remained with me, reading by lamplight in the corner, while Sylvia and Samuel sat with Tommy in his room down the hall in the men's quarters. If Jack shouted, they would hear him.

I slept soundly, but something woke me while it was still dark. A noise in the distance. A thump or crash perhaps. I listened. Sylvia's soft breathing filled the silence. I lit the lamp and held it up to brighten the room. Neither Jack nor Samuel was present.

I strained to hear. Nothing. For several long minutes there were no sounds except that of Sylvia sleeping. She rolled over and stretched an arm across my lap. I lifted it off gently so as not to wake her, just as Jack came in. He saw me and let out a breath.

"What is it?" I whispered. "Was Tate here?"

"Ham."

"Oh God."

Samuel walked in, his fist closed around something. "He ran off."

Sylvia sat up and rubbed her eyes. "What's happened?"

"They frightened Ham away," I said.

She pulled the bed covers up to her chin. Her wide eyes stared at the doorway. "When will it stop?"

"How did you scare it?" I asked the men.

Samuel opened his hand. The amulet lay on his palm. "I showed him this and began to recite the chant Culvert gave us. Ham turned and ran right out the door."

"But I thought the amulet was used to summon the other demon."

"Perhaps it was used for both."

Jack sat on the bed near my feet. "Try to go back to sleep, Hannah. It's the middle of the night."

I lay down, but I didn't think I'd be able to sleep. For one thing, the house creaked and groaned, and for another, Sylvia had effectively wrapped herself around me for reassurance.

I did fall asleep eventually, however. It was light when I awoke again. Jack lay on the mattress on the floor, but I suspected he was awake. I peered down at him and he looked up at me and smiled.

"Good morning," he said.

I yawned. "Good morning. Sleep well?"

"As well as can be expected." If his tired eyes were any indication, he hadn't slept at all. My heart leapt into my throat and I felt so lucky to have him watching over me.

"Thank you. You're my guardian angel."

"And I am your maid," Samuel said, breezing into the room. He set the tray he carried on the table beside the lamp and passed a plate of toast to me and another to Jack. "Eat up, Langley. You'll need your energy."

For demon hunting. I swallowed my first bite of toast and set the rest down. I no longer felt hungry.

***

Sylvia and I watched Samuel, Jack and Bollard leave. Jack had threaded a silver chain through the amulet's hole and wore it around his neck. Both he and Samuel knew the words to the chant by heart. I wasn't sure what use Bollard would be since he couldn't speak, but I suppose an extra pair of hands may be needed to keep the demon at bay while one of the others chanted the incantation.

Staying put in the house was one of the hardest things I'd ever had to do, but of course it was necessary. I didn't feel well enough to be of any real help.

Tommy joined us in the parlor, but we three moved to the scullery to wash dishes. I washed and Sylvia dried. Tommy picked up another towel, but Sylvia ordered him to put it down.

"I have to do something," he said. "Ma'am," he added as an afterthought.

"No, you don't," she snapped. "You're injured."

"It's kind of you to care for me, Miss Langley."

"It's not a kindness. I don't want the plates smashed. You can't do anything useful with only one good arm."

I bit back my laugh. Tommy scowled and sat on a stool. The only thing Sylvia would let him do was tell her where to put the dried dishes.

The small scullery's windows were too high up to look through, unfortunately. I needed to keep watch for Jack and the others or I'd go mad. When the dishes were finally finished, I announced I was going upstairs to one of the bedrooms where the view was better. I was almost at the door when the sound of breaking glass stopped me dead.

"What was that?" Sylvia whispered, coming up behind me.

"Stay here," Tommy ordered.

"No," I said, keeping my voice low.

Sylvia caught his good arm. "You're not going out there."

"I have to see—"

"Tommy." The tremble in her voice made me turn

round. She looked up at the footman, terror in her eyes. "Please stay."

He nodded, albeit reluctantly. "Come away from the door." He grabbed a knife out of a drawer. I thought it a good idea so I took one too. "Hide in the pantry," he ordered both of us.

I backed up to the pantry entrance, Sylvia behind me. Tommy stood at the scullery door and raised the knife.

Footsteps pounded along the floorboards. They grew louder.

Closer.

Ham rushed in, swatting Tommy aside as if he were a fly. Sylvia screamed. Ham came at me. I slashed out, striking him in the chest, but it didn't slow him down. He picked me up and threw me over his shoulder.

Sylvia screamed again. I screamed too and beat the brute with my fists. I clawed at his neck, pulled his hair. If it hurt, he gave no indication. He ran for the door.

Tommy launched himself at Ham's legs as we passed, but the demon kicked him away. Tommy landed awkwardly on his injured arm, face down on the flagstone floor, unconscious.

"Sylvia!" I cried. But it was useless. What could she do? What could any of them do? Jack was gone and the amulet with him. There was no one and nothing to stop the demon.

Sylvia's screams followed me all the way down the hall and out the door.

CHAPTER 14

Ham ran down the steps with me slung over his shoulder like a sack of potatoes. It was an awkward, uncomfortable position. My ribs hurt, my head too as blood rushed to it. I shouted and hammered at his back, but nothing slowed him down. It was hopeless. He was taking me away, and there wasn't a soul who could stop him.

A gunshot fired. I felt Ham flinch, and I thought he'd been struck, but he kept running with me clamped over his shoulder. I looked around, but saw no one. Who'd fired the gun?

Another shot rang out and I glanced up in the direction it had come from—back at the house. Langley was at one of the upstairs windows, a shotgun pointed at the sky. He wasn't firing at us, thank goodness. I was as much a target as the demon.

Why was he firing at all?

I got my answer in the form of Jack and Samuel running out of the woods, Bollard loping behind. Langley had used the gunfire as a signal. Ingenious.

Jack was so fast he reached us well before the others. He punched Ham in the jaw and Ham stumbled, dropping me.

Jack caught me, but quickly let go before the touch became one of desire instead of rescue.

"Run, Hannah!" He ordered as he threw another punch at Ham.

I did, only to stop in my tracks. Reuben Tate came toward me. He wasn't running. Indeed, his steps were labored, as if every one were an effort.

No one else had seen him. Bollard and Samuel had joined in the fight against Ham and were occupied. The demon was strong and every punch inflicted an injury. Tate suddenly stopped walking and looked at the house. At Langley.

Langley stared back. Raised the gun. Aimed.

Tate's Adam's apple bobbed, but he didn't move. He wore no hat and wisps of his white hair waved in the breeze. I held my breath and tensed, waiting for the crack of the gunshot.

None came.

Langley could have shot him if he were accurate enough. Yet he didn't, and I couldn't blame him for that. They'd been friends once. It would take a truly heartless man to kill someone, let alone someone he knew well.

Then I realized he was no longer looking at us, but at the woods. I turned. A scream caught in my throat. The other demon ran toward us at a rapid pace. Langley did fire then, but if the bullet hit the demon, it had no effect. It kept coming.

Tate moved again, faster than before, his face a picture of horror and revulsion. He stumbled twice, falling to his knees. He awkwardly pushed himself up each time with his one hand.

"Jack!" I shouted. "Jack, the other demon!"

"Demon?" Panic pitched Tate's voice high. "Ham! Here! Now!"

Ham obeyed, simply walking away from his opponents. They didn't go after him. All eyes focused on the other demon.

Langley fired again, but it didn't deter the creature. It

wasn't afraid of the noise or of being hit. If any bullets did get their target, it made no difference. The demon kept coming. And coming.

It went for Tate first. He was the closest and the weakest, his missing arm making him more vulnerable. Tate squatted and folded in on himself in an attempt to be as small as possible. "Kill it!" he shouted at Ham.

Ham reached the demon before it got to his master. Then, for some reason, the demon backed away from him. Perhaps it recognized another of the same species and didn't want to fight. Ham was, after all, much bigger, although I doubted he was stronger.

The demon's small eyes settled on me. Unlike Ham, there was no resemblance to anything human in them. They were yellow and small, set wide apart. I saw no trace of the spirits of the children.

Fear turned my legs to jelly. My heart flapped wildly. I stumbled back, put my arms up to defend myself.

"Hannah!" Jack shouted.

Heat and fire roared past me. A fireball slammed into the demon, but had little impact. Unlike the first few times, it didn't scurry away. It had learned that fire couldn't hurt it.

"Hannah!" The shout came from Tate this time.

Jack grasped the amulet hanging from his neck and began the chant. The demon's eyes widened. It turned on him. Ran. Jack spoke faster.

The demon swiped at him, sending him to the ground.

"Jack!" I screamed.

He pushed himself up, stumbled and fell again with a grunt. "Amulet," he said on a groan.

It lay a few feet away in the mud. Samuel dove for it and began the chant anew. The demon raced at him and Samuel threw the amulet at Bollard. He caught it, but Samuel continued the chant.

The demon seemed confused at first, then must have decided Bollard was the weakest. It smashed a first into his face and Bollard crumpled to the ground. The amulet tumbled out of his grip.

Jack scrambled for it, but again the demon attacked. It pounced on him. Jack rolled and kicked out, striking it in its middle. Samuel continued to chant.

A muscular arm snaked around my waist and hefted me up. Ham!

Jack hadn't noticed. He and Samuel were busy fending off the demon and trying to send it back. I swallowed my scream. I didn't dare distract them.

"Get her away," Tate snarled at Ham.

I hadn't seen him up close in weeks, and the change in him was profound. Sweat made the hair at his temples damp. Dark shadows circled sunken eyes amid his pale face. He looked deathly. I wondered how long he had left.

How long I had.

I struggled against Ham, even though I knew it was useless. He was too strong. I kicked and scratched anyway and would have bitten him if he didn't hold me from behind.

"Come with me willingly," Tate suddenly said. "With your help, I might find a cure in time."

I stopped fighting and stared back at him. "Why did you do this to me? To yourself?" I wanted to scream at him that I'd been only a baby, but there was no point now. It was done, and I needed to save my energy.

"Many reasons." He glanced past me to Jack and the others. I dared not look. The demon's snarling and Samuel's chanting told me it wasn't yet over. "Come with me, Miss Smith."

My breaths came in short, sharp bursts. Ham held me tight, but didn't squeeze. I didn't feel tired, but I did feel weak. Useless. I hated it. "What will happen if I do?"

He glanced past me again. We both knew now was not the time for this discussion. "Just come with me!" he snapped. "Ham, go."

"No!" Jack cried out in anguish from behind me.

I turned, thinking he was watching Ham drag me away, but his attention was entirely on the other demon. It held the amulet between its claw-like hands and snapped it in half. Samuel finished the chant.

Nothing happened.

The demon's mouth split into what could have been a grin, but was little more than a stretch of the slit in its face. It tossed the pieces of the amulet away.

Oh God. What now?

Nobody moved. We were all too stunned. Our one chance lay broken and useless in the mud. The demon knew it too. It went for Jack.

I screamed.

"We have to get away," Tate said to Ham.

Ham dragged me off. I dug my heels into the ground, but my attempts were pathetic.

I watched as Jack managed to punch the demon over and over, but it had little effect and he was tiring quickly. I could see it in the way he stood, his shoulders not quite so square, his chest rising and falling with his hard breathing.

Bollard joined him, but he wasn't as fast or capable as Jack and the demon easily swatted him away.

Then Samuel spoke. "Look at me." His voice was compelling, smooth as silk.

I looked away, tried to break the compulsion to sink into his voice and do as he said. It wasn't easy, but I managed.

"Look into my eyes and listen to my voice," Samuel intoned.

The demon looked. Then it smashed its fist into the side of Samuel's face. His eyes rolled up, his lids fluttered closed, and he fell to the ground.

The demon turned on Jack. It swung at him. Jack ducked and spun so sharply that the contents of his pocket emptied into the mud. He got up and threw a punch at the demon, but he wasn't moving as fast as usual. He was exhausted. It was only a matter of time now. The demon would win. We had nothing to defeat it.

Oh Jack. God no. Please, please no.

Ham, Tate and I reached the edge of the lawn. I resisted

all the way so our progress wasn't as fast as Tate would have liked. He urged Ham to run. The brute still held me around the waist, leaving my legs loose so that I was able to trip him. We tumbled to the ground, and he let me go. But only for a moment and not long enough for me to escape. He picked me up and swung me over his shoulder again.

I hung upside down. My cap had fallen off back in the scullery and my long hair skimmed the brute's thighs. I twisted and fought him, but it was no good. I began to cry, great wracking sobs that I couldn't control. Jack was going to die, and I was going to become another test for a madman.

"Bollard!" Jack shouted. "The knife!"

I looked up to see Jack catch the small knife he'd been carrying lately. It must have fallen out of his pocket. It wouldn't kill the demon, but perhaps it would slow it down.

The demon barreled toward him. Bollard jumped on it and Samuel too from the other side. But the demon kept going, on and on toward Jack. Just as it reached him, Jack stepped neatly aside and thrust the knife into its chest.

It stumbled and fell, taking Bollard and Samuel down with it. They scrambled up. The demon did not.

Then it did the most peculiar thing. It let out a piercing cry and began to disintegrate. It was like watching a pile of sawdust blow away in the wind. Within seconds, there was nothing left.

I gasped out a cry of relief.

Jack, still breathing hard, turned to us and ran. We had stopped to watch the demon dying, the sight mesmerizing everyone, but the sight of Jack approaching at speed set Ham going again. Tate too.

Jack was fast. I renewed my own efforts to release myself, kicking and hitting Ham to try to slow him down. It was working too. It worked so well that when Ham looked back, he stumbled and fell.

I landed on my hands and knees, mostly unharmed. I scurried out of his reach, but it didn't matter. He didn't try to grab me. He'd already got up and was facing down Jack.

Ham was clearly the stronger, and Jack was obviously weary, yet his supreme speed meant he dodged several of Ham's punches. It also meant he could duck and drive the knife into his opponent's body.

Ham's eyes widened. He began to disintegrate into dust, just as the other demon had done. It was all over in a moment. Ham was gone.

Tate too. He must have slipped into the woods while we were occupied.

Jack knelt in the mud beside me. "Hannah," he gasped out. "Hannah...are you all right?"

I nodded and dragged in deep breaths. I may not have worked hard, but my chest hurt from lack of air.

He pressed his lips together and clasped and unclasped the knife in his fist as if he were undecided about something. Then he pulled me into a brief, powerful embrace. Heat blasted me from the inside. Fire shot from my hands and Jack's too, only to extinguish in the damp grass and mud.

We sprang apart. I breathed heavily, trying to regain my composure. He swore and punched the ground with his fist.

"Jack," I said. "You did it. You killed both demons."

Samuel and Bollard came up to us. They looked as terrible as Jack. Hair messy, covered in mud, and bruises and cuts on their faces and knuckles. They both bent over and sucked air into their lungs.

"Wait here," Jack said, standing. "I'm going after Tate."

"Be careful," I called out to him as he ran off. "He may have a gun."

"He would have used it on us if he did," Samuel said, following Jack. Only Bollard remained with me, and I was grateful not to be left entirely on my own.

I couldn't take my eyes off the woods. I scanned the trees, looking for danger. My ears strained for any sounds, but the woods were silent. Bollard and I stood side by side, watching and waiting. I expected him to return to the house, but he didn't.

Eventually, after what seemed an eternity, Jack and

Samuel returned. Without Tate.

"He's gone," Samuel said when he reached us. "We found hoof prints in the soil. He must have ridden away."

"Bloody hell," Jack bit off. He kicked the ground, gouging out a clump of muddy grass.

"At least Ham is gone," I said. "Tate won't have anyone to help him now. If that amulet belonged to him, it's useless." Yet I doubted that Tate had summoned the second demon. He seemed surprised to see it, nor could he control it the way he could control Ham. "Do you think it was Tate's doing?"

"We may never know," Jack said darkly.

Samuel cast a resigned look in the direction in which Tate had run off. "Going by his reaction, I wonder if he's innocent on that score."

"That means someone else summoned it," I said. "Who? And why?"

Nobody had an answer to that. The dreadfulness of the thought threatened to overshadow our victories, so I changed the subject. "How could that little knife kill those things?"

"I was wondering the same thing," Samuel said.

We didn't get an opportunity to discuss it. "Hannah!" Sylvia shouted from one of the windows. "Hannah, Jack, come back inside."

"We should do as she says," I said.

Jack glanced into the woods then down at the knife in his hand. It was the one with the beautifully carved handle that had been given to him by his parents. The only thing he had left from them, so he'd once told me.

We walked—or limped—back to the house and made our way to the parlor. Sylvia and Langley met us there.

"Tommy?" I asked. "Is he…?"

"What happened to Tommy?" Jack said, rising from the chair again.

"I'm here," Tommy said, entering. He balanced a tray on his good arm, a teapot with three cups and saucers on it. A large bump bulged on his temple.

"Are you all right?" I asked. "You were out cold when I left."

He gave me a lopsided smile. "I've a bit of a headache, Miss Smith, thanks for asking."

"He just came to not long ago," Sylvia said with a scowl. "He was in no condition to come and help. Nor should he have been near hot things yet."

Tommy paused and squeezed his eyes shut. The tray tilted dangerously to the side and Jack took it off him. "Sylvia's right," he said, setting it down on the table near me. "You should be resting. Besides, I need something stronger than tea."

"Already here." Tommy nodded at the smaller table near the window where a decanter and glasses sat. He rubbed his head and winced.

"Sit down," Langley snapped. "You're making everyone uncomfortable. You too, Bollard."

Tommy sat, but Bollard did not. In fact, he signed something to Langley then left us altogether. Langley watched him go with an unreadable expression.

"You killed them," Sylvia said, pouring tea. Her hand was surprisingly steady considering what she'd just witnessed. Usually merely uttering the word kill would have her trembling, but she seemed as steady as someone with more fortitude. "I saw from Uncle's window. How?"

Jack pulled the knife out of his pocket again. "I stabbed them both with this."

"But I thought knives couldn't harm demons."

Samuel handed Jack a tumbler of brandy and offered another to Tommy. For once, Tommy took it without hesitation. Langley accepted a cup of tea from Sylvia. "Let me have a look," Samuel said.

Jack passed him the knife. He turned it over and rubbed his thumb down the blade. "It's a good-looking piece. I like the detail in the handle. It would have taken a lot of skill to carve such an intricate pattern. But I don't see how it could have killed Ham and that other creature. It's quite small for one thing."

"Do you think Mr. Culvert was wrong?" Sylvia asked.

"What exactly did he say about how to kill a demon?" Langley held out his hand for the knife and Jack passed it to him.

"He said a special incantation needed to be spoken while holding the amulet," Jack said. "It should send the demon back."

"Nothing could kill it?"

My gaze locked with Jack's. "A blade forged in the Otherworld," I said.

He stared back at me. Blinked.

"You said your parents gave that to you."

He nodded and took the knife back from Langley. He touched a finger to the point. "It's the only thing I have from them."

Sylvia lowered her cup to her saucer. The clatter was loud in the heavy silence. "How did they come to possess a blade forged in the Otherworld?"

We all looked to Langley, but he merely shrugged. "I can assure you I don't know the answer. I am as intrigued as you are."

"Thank God you have it," Samuel muttered. "Or we would have been…you know."

Jack drained his glass and filled it again from the decanter.

"Interesting," Langley said, as if he were observing the results of an experiment. "Whoever is keeping watch on Hannah must have the knife on them at all times in case Tate summons another demon."

"I'll be the one protecting her," Jack said. He spoke as if it were a given and not open for debate.

Yet that is what Langley did. "Samuel is capable too."

Samuel looked as surprised by the suggestion as Jack. "Of course I'll relieve him whenever necessary, but I'm sure he'll want to be the one with her most of the time."

205

"Thank you, Gladstone," Jack said quietly. "And thanks for your help out there. You would make a formidable opponent in a fair fight."

Samuel went to say something, but Langley cut him off. "If you wish to remain in this house, you'll watch Hannah when I ask you to."

"Er, yes. Of course." Samuel gave an apologetic shrug to Jack. He scowled back, then fixed a brutally blunt glare on his uncle.

Langley turned his wheelchair around and rolled out of the parlor. I was quite certain now that he was attempting to push Samuel and me together. I felt saddened, although I didn't really know why. It didn't matter what he wanted or ordered us to do. Our hearts dictated to us, not him. And yet I wanted him to understand the depth of feeling between Jack and I. Wanted him to accept it.

The tension remained after he left. I think we were all waiting to see what Jack would do. In the end, Sylvia was the one who broke the silence.

"You all need baths," she announced with a wrinkle of her nose.

There were two baths in Frakingham. One was located in a bathing room in the damaged part of the house, and another in the butler's pantry. That one had to be carried upstairs by the servants to our bedrooms and filled from pails. We would have to take turns.

"You first," Samuel said to me.

"Come with me to the lake, Hannah," Jack said suddenly.

Sylvia gasped. "No! I absolutely forbid it."

"We'll stay in the shallows. It'll be quite safe."

"She may be safe from drowning," Sylvia said, hand on hip, "but have you forgotten about Tate?"

"Propriety be damned. As to Tate, he won't come near us for a while. He's weak and alone. Besides, if he summons another demon, I'll use this again." He indicated the knife in his pocket. "Well, Hannah?"

I nodded. "All right."

***

We carried towels down to the lake. We both kept our eyes peeled for Tate, but there was no sign of him. As we passed the spot on the lawn where Jack had killed the demon, I paused to look for any trace of it. There was none.

"I wonder how your parents got a hold of that knife," I said.

"I don't know. I don't even know if it came from them."

"Oh? I thought you said it did."

"It's what I've always believed." He shrugged. "But it could have been given to me by anyone when I was baby."

"Do you think Langley was telling the truth when he said he knows nothing about it?"

"Who knows anything for certain about Langley? Except perhaps Bollard." He looked down at the churned up mud and grass near where the demon had died. "I'm just relieved that it's gone."

"Me too." We set off again for the lake. "What do you think happened to the souls of the children it consumed?"

He lifted his face to the gray sky as if he could find them there. "I don't know. I hope they got out somehow. We'll write to Mrs. Beaufort and ask her. She may know."

"We ought to tell the Beauforts and Culverts anyway. They'll want to know what happened."

"I suspect Culvert will want to see the blade too."

We reached the edge of the lake and placed our towels on a grassy patch. Jack removed his shoes and indicated I should do the same. He then removed his waistcoat, but left his shirt and trousers on.

"Are you going to wear all of that in?" he asked with a nod at my dress.

I cast a glance back at the house.

"Don't worry about Sylvia," he said.

"I'm more concerned about Langley."

"Forget him too."

"That's not easy to do. He won't like this. He doesn't seem to want us to be...together."

"I don't care what he does and doesn't want where you're concerned. He won't throw either of us out, if that's what you're afraid of."

My protest died on my lips. I *had* been worried I realized. "I don't want to leave Frakingham," I said. "Or you."

His smile started out as surprised and quickly softened to reassuring, melting my heart. "If you ever do leave, I'm coming with you."

Tears pricked the backs of my eyes. I was too stunned to speak.

He backed into the lake and beckoned me. "Come in, Hannah. It's freezing."

The water lapped at my stockinged feet then my knees. He kept wading backward until he was waist deep. I followed until I was in up to my thighs. The lake bottom was pebbly and sandy, the water clear. I could see my toes.

"Cold?" he asked.

"Yes," I said. "It's lovely." Cold water and air had always felt good, but this time it felt even better. The icy water soothed my hot skin and cleared my mind. For the first time in a week, I felt more alert, not at all tired. "It's like medicine. I feel...cured."

But we both knew I wasn't cured. When I got out of the lake, I would feel unwell again. At least I knew I could always come to the lake if the heat ever became too much.

Jack disappeared beneath the surface and came up again a moment later. He moaned. "That's better."

"Your cuts hurt?" I asked.

"A little." Knowing Jack, that was code for 'a lot.' "The water soothes them," he added. "Come in further. Put your whole body in."

I walked until I too was in up to my waist. My skirts billowed on the surface and the stones underfoot became slippery. "I can't swim."

"Just a little more then put your face under."

I took a step toward him, and another, and soon the water was up to my chest. I tried to push my skirt down, but it kept floating up again. Damnation.

Jack laughed.

"I'm glad you find this amusing," I said.

"Here, let me help."

"No, if Langley sees…" I stepped back and slipped. I went under the water. My feet struggled to find purchase on the pebbles. I flapped my arms, but my skirt got in the way. It was around my head, weighing me down, holding me under.

Panicked, I opened my mouth to scream. Water rushed in and up my nose. I couldn't see, couldn't breathe.

Then two strong arms grabbed me and pulled me to the surface. I coughed and spluttered in Jack's face, but he didn't let go. He held me, rubbing my back until the coughs subsided. I clung to him. Our bodies pressed together from chest to hip, our arms wrapped around each other. We were as close as we'd ever been…and nothing happened.

No sparks, no fire, no heat. Well, perhaps a little heat, but not to an alarming level.

He realized it too and caught my face in his hands. "Hannah," he murmured. His eyes blazed brightly, his face filled with wonder. "Do you know what this means?"

"The cold water cools us enough so that we can touch."

He nodded. "It also means I can do this."

He kissed me. His lips were so soft, yet his mouth urgent. Hungry. It was like we were in a fever, tasting and teasing. I pressed my hands to the back of his head, holding him. He wound my hair around his fingers and held on as if his life depended upon it. My heart pounded in my chest, and I thought it would burst out. I didn't care. I just wanted to taste Jack's kisses.

"Hannah," he murmured without fully breaking the kiss. "You're so perfect." He circled both arms around me and clung tight.

Speaking of perfection—I wanted to touch him all over, feel every inch of hard muscle that I'd been dreaming about for weeks. I ran my hands over his shoulders, across his chest. I tore at his shirt, popping the buttons, and dove inside. He groaned against my lips.

"We have to stop," he gasped out, "or I'll never forgive myself."

I didn't want to stop. I knew what would happen if we kept going, and I wanted it. Wanted to feel all of him, be with him. I knew it was wrong and I didn't care. How could I when it felt so right?

I took his hand and placed it on my breast. Shocks of heat tore through me. A spark shot from Jack's fingers and sizzled in the water.

He stepped back with a yelp and let me go. I plunged my hot hands under and steam rose in wisps.

The moment dragged while we both caught our breaths. "Well," I finally said. "It would seem ice-cold water only works to a certain point."

He turned around sharply and groaned. "This is going to kill me, Hannah. Not being able to touch you…"

"We can touch," I said. "We'll just have to make sure it doesn't go so far next time."

He groaned again, louder. "Easier said than done."

"Yes," I muttered, staring down at my hands. I felt leaden, tired, and misery threatened to overwhelm me. I closed my eyes and forced all sad thoughts away. I could not afford to spend even a moment feeling sorry for myself when I had so much to be thankful for. I had Jack.

He turned around and gave me one of his sad smiles. "Thank you, Hannah."

"What for?"

"For trusting me and coming into the lake."

"I almost drowned."

"I won't let anything happen to you. That's a promise."

A lump clogged my throat. Swallowing and talking became impossible, so I nodded.

"We *will* find a cure," he said. "We have to, because I refuse to lose you."

My lip wobbled and I hugged myself. All I could manage

was another nod. He'd never sounded so convinced of my recovery and I didn't want to say anything to bring back his doubts.

He held out his hand and I took it. There were no sparks. The heat of the moment had dissipated along with its intensity, and the icy water was once more acting as a balm. "Let's go back inside," he said. "I'm sure Sylvia has her lecture all prepared for us by now."

"You think she was watching?"

"You can be sure of it."

"In that case," I said. "Give me one more kiss. We might as well make the lecture worth her while and ours."

He did.

THE END

LOOK OUT FOR

Heart Burn

The third book in the first FREAK HOUSE TRILOGY.

Will Hannah and Jack ever find peace together? Find out in the heart-stopping final installment of the 1st Freak House Trilogy.

To be notified when C.J. has a new release, sign up to her newsletter. Send an email to cjarcher.writes@gmail.com

Interact with the characters from Freak House on Tumblr.
http://freakhouseresidents.tumblr.com

ABOUT THE AUTHOR

C.J. Archer has loved history and books for as long as she can remember. She worked as a librarian and technical writer until she was able to channel her twin loves by writing historical fiction. She has won and placed in numerous romance writing contests, including taking home RWAustralia's Emerald Award in 2008 for the manuscript that would become her novel *Honor Bound*. Under the name Carolyn Scott, she has published contemporary romantic mysteries, including *Finders Keepers Losers Die*, and *The Diamond Affair*. After spending her childhood surrounded by the dramatic beauty of outback Queensland, she lives today in suburban Melbourne, Australia, with her husband and their two children.

She loves to hear from readers. You can contact her in one of these ways:
Website: www.cjarcher.com
Email: cjarcher.writes@gmail.com
Facebook: www.facebook.com/CJArcherAuthorPage